He'd never feared death, but he hadn't spent much time thinking about it, either. For the first time since arriving here, the black reality of his death leered at him.

His only defense seemed to be to stay alert, but he had to fight to keep from blacking out.

He yanked himself awake.

Like a drowning man, he struggled up again.

When he started going under once more, he thought that he may have been weakened too much to fight off the end for a third time.

Then a tremendous explosion rocked the earth, jolting Durell wide-eyed . . .

ASSIGNMENT: DEATH SHIP

WILL B. AARONS

FAWCETT GOLD MEDAL • NEW YORK

A Fawcett Gold Medal Book
Published by Ballantine Books

Library of Congress Catalog Card Number: 83-90037

ISBN 0-449-12440-1

Manufactured in the United States of America

First Ballantine Books Edition: October 1983

Chapter 1

Durell squinted into the Caribbean glare, searching the distance where the stricken liner *Sun Rover* could be expected to emerge from its shroud of salt haze. A Coast Guard cutter would be there, too, the *Henry*.

They were being called death ships, floating tombs, but no one really knew why. Nor would they know until Durell and John Nelson and Maj. Charles P. Miller set foot on their decks.

En route to St. Thomas after an overnight stay in San Juan, the *Sun Rover* had reported no problems, until a garbled transmission called on the Coast Guard to render emergency medical assistance. Despite repeated queries, its radio remained silent after that single call. Nearly the same had happened to the cutter. Its helicopter had flown west to Roosevelt Roads Naval Station in Puerto Rico, picked up a medical team, landed on the *Sun Rover*, and fallen silent. All that was known after that was the *Henry* had arrived on the scene and dispatched a boat to investigate—and had not been heard from since.

1

Durell glanced back into the helicopter's shadowed cabin. The crew-cut, hard-jawed Nelson waited in grim readiness beside Chuck Miller, a paunchy man of fifty with a round, fatherly face and thoughtful eyes. Maj. Miller lifted his brows. Durell shrugged, not sure what he was questioning. Nelson stared out the window.

Durell was chief field agent for K Section, an anonymous splinter of the clandestine services that formed the trouble-shooting arm of the CIA. Nelson was a junior field officer in the same agency.

Durell watched the horizon and exhaled slowly to dispel the anxiety he felt. It was a brilliantly sunny day, with visibility limited to about ten miles by haze. Durell's was one of three Navy SH-3H choppers flying in V formation. The other two were along to observe and assist in returning survivors to Puerto Rico—if there were any.

Aerial surveillance had followed loss of contact with the *Henry*. Durell had seen the photos upon his arrival at Roosevelt Roads.

The decks were littered with bodies.

And no one knew what had happened, or how, or why.

Could be as many as a thousand victims. . . .

The copilot tapped Durell's shoulder and pointed into the haze on the horizon, drawing his attention to two vague, linear shapes that were the stricken ships. Durell pointed them out to Nelson and Maj. Miller.

"They looked perfectly normal from here," Nelson observed.

"But something happened—something that apparently killed everyone aboard," Maj. Miller said.

Durell watched the approaching ships. "Finding out what it was is only the beginning. Who caused it is the next question."

"Terrorists." It was Nelson, his jaw hard. "The world's full of people willing to kill for attention."

"Never on this scale," Durell replied. "No one's taken responsibility."

"I wager they'll crow before the day is over, the devils," Maj. Miller growled, tapping an empty pipe on his palm in emphasis. He wiped flakes of black crust on his jumpsuit.

2

Durell waited and worried. His would be the third party to board the *Sun Rover*, and the first to come back alive—if he were lucky.

He was a big man with a lean and agile build. His eyes were the color of blue-black storm clouds, and the stormier his temper, the blacker they got. Despite the countless hazards he'd survived, the split-second judgments that had meant the difference between life and death—sometimes death, and he had to live with that, too—his face was youthful. His thick mat of black hair held only a sprinkling of gray at the temples. His grandpa Jonathan had reared him a gambler and a hunter, with a beached riverboat his home and the Louisiana bayous his stalking ground. The lessons had served him well in a game, covering the world, with stakes as high as they could get.

The two ships were much nearer now. They shone like ghosts, their white sides radiating foreboding as they drifted.

"Ready with the suits?" Durell asked calmly.

"Roger, Sam," Maj. Miller replied. Lovingly, he raised a silver-colored suit designed to cover a man from head to toe for protection from biological or chemical agents. Built into the hood was a breathing mask shaped like a rat's nose, with enormous round goggles. "Get into this, and I'll check you over," he said. He also gave one to Nelson.

When all three of them were clad in the baggy garments, they tested the built-in transceivers and looked each other over. Durell's suit was cumbersome; the freon-cooled air of its self-contained breathing pack chilled the sweat around his collar and under his armpits, and it smelled of rubber. He felt the weight of an autonomous transmitter in a pocket on his sleeve. It would radio continuous readings of the suit's interior environment, plus his pulse and respiration, to a console in one of the other helicopters. In case he was overcome while alone, the others could be alerted and perhaps save his life. Of course, the suit was meant to preclude any problems, but he didn't mind the backup. Maj. Miller was familiar with the gear. All NASA spinoffs. Durell was content to let him be the expert.

The major was more scientist than soldier, having earned a doctorate in biochemistry from MIT. A bachelor, he'd spent most of his working life in laboratories. On the flight from Washington, he had told Durell that women were the cause of most of the troubles in the world. "Science," he'd added with a chuckle, "has caused most of the rest."

Durell hadn't pursued it.

"Look. We're passing over the cutter," Nelson said.

The three looked down, then at each other after the *Henry* had flashed by. "Must have been twenty, thirty men lying on the deck," Maj. Miller said. "What's the *Henry*'s complement?"

"Fifteen officers and a hundred forty-nine men," Durell said. "If the rest were all right, the dead would be off the deck by now."

"Whatever hit them must have been brought back from the *Sun Rover* by their boarding party," Maj. Miller said.

Durell said, "Maybe they found a canister of poison gas or nerve gas—something really lethal, like Sarin—and took it back and accidentally popped the cork."

"Maybe," Maj. Miller said. He was thoughtful. "I certainly know of no disease that kills so quickly."

"If it's gas, it'll be dispersed by now, but what if it is a disease?" Durell asked. "The chopper crews aren't protected, and they'll have to get in close to drop us off; couldn't they catch something from germs in the air?"

"Most germs don't live long in air and sunlight, Sam. They've got to have an organic medium, whether it's a body or a body's excretions, humus, filthy water—it depends on what kind of bacteria it is, of course." Maj. Miller took a breath. "Some sort of pathogen could have been blown through the ship's ventilating system initially, but only by quickly finding host organisms—the bodies of the passengers—could it have survived."

"But the Henry's boarding party—" Durell began.

"Undoubtedly tried to aid the passengers, touched them, their body products, breathed their exhalations—remember, a

4

sneeze throws out millions of germs, although most of them may survive only briefly," Maj. Miller said.

"Then you think it was a germ?" asked Nelson. He liked things pinned down.

"My God, man, how could it have been? There *is* no germ that could have done that," Maj. Miller said.

Nelson blinked at the outburst, then turned his hardened face back to the window.

Durell heard the helicopter's rotor make a flat whacking noise as they began to hover. They were over their destination. The pilot's voice came through the headset. "It looks mighty grim, gentlemen," he announced.

A crewman opened the door and assisted Durell with the sling he would ride down to the deck. "Nelson, you come next," he said, and swung into the air and down. Five hundred miles north of Venezuela, it was a perfect Caribbean afternoon—until he looked down. The sight brought a bitter taste to the back of his tongue.

Bloating corpses littered the hot decks of the luxury liner. He noticed the women first, in their gaudy holiday dresses with the sun shining on their wind-tossed hair. Both sexes were scattered everywhere, many in contorted poses, knees drawn up tightly from their last moments of agony. Few huddled together, as if pain had blotted out any pretty thoughts of accompanying each other into death and left them writhing alone, like poisoned ants. Here and there Durell picked out the white uniforms of ship personnel. All in the same awkward attitudes of strewn mannequins. In the emerald water of the swimming pool corpses floated or lay darkly against the bottom, fully clothed.

Among the hundreds of figures, not one stirred.

Lowered slowly through the turbulent air, he thought how the *Sun Rover's* winter-weary passengers—mostly from the New York City region—must have thought they were living a sunny dream—until it had turned into a nightmare.

He glanced at the chronometer strapped to his wrist: barely six hours had passed since the ship's sole call for assistance.

The captain must have waited too long to request help, when minutes had counted. By the time the signal was authorized, it already was too late.

The American public knew nothing of this, Durell remembered. Maybe it never would. Sugar Cube and the joint chiefs had been kept posted hourly.

Behind the frost-coated windows of the nation's capital the top levels of government had been jolted by the tragedy. Hurried meetings and hushed conferences had been convened in the greatest secrecy.

How could such loss of life have been engineered?

Who had perpetrated it?

Why?

The leaders of America waited in their plush Washington offices for the other shoe to fall. . . .

Durell waited beneath the hovering helicopter until Nelson came down beside him. He liked Nelson, who was young and ambitious and seemed to spend more nights with dossiers and training manuals than with his petite wife. There wasn't a manual for everything, but Durell hadn't told him that; he'd have to get more years of experience under his belt before he'd be ready to believe it.

The enveloping suit made the scene beyond Durell's goggles a dreamlike one of flags fluttering silently in a breeze he couldn't feel. Gulls wheeled. A ship's newspaper flapped past his feet.

Nelson's voice was edgy. "I'll start below decks," he said.

"Right. I'll head upstairs. I'm making an announcement on the PA, so there's no need to look in every room. Just get through it; get the pictures. Any survivors can assemble on the foredeck."

"Survivors? Sure." His tone was sarcastic, doubtful. Then he added, "It's a big ship; I can't believe they're going to send her to the bottom."

"They can't take a chance on contaminating a port."

Durell sounded matter-of-fact. "Better get moving. There isn't much time." He watched Nelson pick his way through the bodies that littered the deck. Vision, especially downward vision, was poor in these masks. Nelson's silvery form reminded him of some sort of graveyard apparition among the dead.

"Maj. Miller?" Durell called.

"Yo, Cajun." The scientist used Durell's code name.

"Come down for your samples when you get the all-clear. Should be shortly." The threat of attack was only a distant possibility, but the major was too valuable to risk.

"How about now? I have work to do."

"You'll get it done," Durell said. He started for the bridge, a feeling of threat weighing against him. Death was all around, with no visible cause. The suit was cumbersome and heavy; it made him feel vulnerable. Climbing stairs in the boxy shoes was difficult. The ocean shimmered far below; his airpack chilled the sweat popping out on his brow. Gulls made white trails around the black-topped funnel, where thin smoke still swirled. But the vessel had no motion at all.

The eerie feeling persisted—he took comfort from the heavy .45 automatic strapped to his hip, even though his usual weapon was a snub-nosed .38 S&W revolver.

Nelson's flat voice came through the earphone. "God! Vomit and shit everywhere. We aren't going to find anyone alive on this tub, Cajun."

"Just keep looking. Are you getting the pictures?"

"Sure, but I don't know who'd want to see them."

"You're not taking them for the six o'clock news," Durell said.

The photos would be a record for secret archives buried deep in the Virginia countryside. They might not be made public for a hundred years, if then; or, if there should be a criminal trial, they could be submitted as evidence.

The ship and all it held would be long gone.

Durell put all his weight against the wheelhouse door and shoved. He found a dead deck officer blocking it; the helmsman was crumpled behind the wheel. The captain was alone in his quarters, lying on the floor. His knees were drawn up and his elbows were turned in over his belly, almost touching, as if to fend off cramping. The blotched flesh of his face held the remains of a grimace; the whites of his eyes showed a bloodshot yellow.

Durell's measured breathing sounded in his ears. The deck trembled minutely to vibrations from machinery far below.

There was no clue to the disaster in the log.

He thumbed the PA switch, announced for survivors to assemble on the foredeck, then began working his way through staterooms, lounges, restaurants, deck by deck, moving swiftly.

Nothing happened.

"Maj. Miller?" he called.

"I'm still waiting." He sounded annoyed.

"You may come down now."

Durell kept moving, knowing that Maj. Miller knew what to do. Since taking corpses ashore presented an unacceptable degree of hazard to the health of the populace, the scientist would collect tissue and blood samples on board and deliver them to agency pathologists. He would also attempt to find the source of whatever it was that had killed these people.

Durell stepped past a fallen steward.

Victims slumped where they had died sitting against the corridor wall.

Nelson's voice broke the silence. "Infirmary's full, all dead."

"I read. Keep moving," Durell replied.

"Right. I'm getting the willies. Let's get finished," Nelson said. "Must have been some panic down here. I found a piece of a dress snagged on an open porthole. I guess she must have jumped."

Durell looked grimly about him, at the grandparents and honeymooners, the lovers real and hopeful who last night had danced in San Juan moonlight.

Their teeth gleamed dryly.

Maj. Miller's words came through. "I've found it; it's in

the ventilating system, sure enough. There's a timer, a bottle fixed with a spray nozzle, and a fired CO_2 cartridge. It blew the solution in there and it was all over the ship in no time."

Nelson spoke. "Solution of what?"

"Wouldn't we all like to know," Durell said. Directing his words to the other, he said: "Bag it, major. Good work."

"It must be incredibly potent. The whole apparatus fits in my palm," Maj. Miller said. He sounded admiring in spite of himself—and a bit fearful.

Durell addressed the pilot of the helicopter. "You may lower the specimen locker." Then, to Maj. Miller: "Got your slides yet, major?"

"Roger."

"Very well. Everybody to the foredeck." He felt the grip of tension begin to loosen. The *Sun Rover* was accursed, but at least his party would leave it alive. He had been taking stairs two steps at a time when Nelson's voice suddenly stopped him.

"Hello!" There was surprised disbelief in the word.

Durell waited in suspense.

"I won't harm you; what are you hiding?" Nelson said.

Durell broke in. "Who do you have, Nelson? Where are you?" He was apprehensive.

"A survivor," Nelson replied. "Pretty, too. I don't think the sight of this bio-chem suit is helping, though. She looks scared crazy. Freaked out." His voice became tense, coaxing. "Give it to me. Give it here, miss. She's got a knife. . . ."

"Be careful," Durell said. "Don't try to disarm her until I get there." He looked back and forth through the big goggles, annoyed by their limited vision, twisting his shoulders awkwardly. "I said where are you," he repeated.

"I can handle it, Cajun."

Durell heard a hard gasp, a distant, muted cry which must have come from the woman, and Nelson's panting. "I got her. We're coming up." There was something in his voice. . . .

"Are you all right?" Durell asked.

"I got a little cut on the arm. Just a scratch." He spoke lightly, but his voice shook.

Durell cursed silently. He could do nothing more. He went and stood below the beating blades of the helicopter, waiting for the others, wondering what would happen to Nelson. Maybe nothing. Maybe whatever had wiped out life here had done its work and died, or dissipated in the air. Maybe—by some miracle—the knife wasn't contaminated. He also remembered that Maj. Miller carried a selection of antidotes for just this eventuality. They could only shoot Nelson full of them and hope for the best.

A specimen locker dangled beneath the helicopter, awaiting the arrival of Maj. Miller. It would be decontaminated, along with everything else, before being hauled into the aircraft. Every possibility of contaminating the helicopter had been guarded against, even to the extent of changing and showering in a chamber lowered by a support chopper before leaving the ship.

Maj. Miller came out of the superstructure. Durell saw the concern in his eyes, even through the goggles. The scientist held up two bags, showing them to Durell. One was for tissue and blood samples, the other for the spraying mechanism. He placed them in the specimen locker and signaled for it to be cranked up to the helicopter.

"No idea what was in the bottle?" Durell asked.

"None, sorry to say. Only a laboratory investigation will come up with an answer."

They avoided the obvious topic, aware that Nelson could hear them over their intercom. They didn't want to say anything that might panic him. The looks they exchanged were enough to express their deep worry.

"What about the woman?" Durell asked. "If a disease is involved, can she spread it?"

"Possibly."

"Even if she doesn't get sick herself?"

"It's highly unlikely, but she could be a carrier. We mustn't take chances," Maj. Miller said. "She'll have to be isolated. Same for Nelson."

"I heard that. I'm all right," Nelson interjected.

At that moment Durell caught a flicker of movement in the shadows of a doorway, then saw Nelson emerge with the woman held firmly by her upper arm.

"Here they come. Bitch!" Maj. Miller said.

She looked dazed and drawn, and her walk was unsteady. She was thin and pretty, with wide-set brown eyes and a mane of thick, copper-red hair parted on the side and falling freely in loose curls. Durell guessed her age at twenty-five. She wore a knit sweater and pleated skirt printed boldly in shades of red, white, and violet. She had lost her shoes.

"I'll take her," Durell said. "Get your shots." He motioned to Maj. Miller.

"I feel perfectly fine," Nelson insisted. But there was a plea for reassurance in his tone. He held out his arm.

"Sit down. This will have to go into the thigh," Maj. Miller told him. He didn't waste any time, but jabbed the needle of a disposable syringe right through the bio-chem suit. "There's some more," Durell heard him say.

Durell called for the decontamination module to be lowered to the deck. It would be left behind to go down with the *Sun Rover*.

The woman screamed.

It was a primordial, gut-wringing howl that turned Durell's spine to ice. She whirled on him, flailing with her fists, and Durell got her in a bear hug, pinning her arms against her sides. She struggled with the unnatural fury of madness, baring teeth in a contorted face. Then she stopped as abruptly as she had begun.

Maj. Miller was guiding the big fiberglass module onto the deck, troubled somewhat by freshening breezes, and Durell felt it thump down, saw the lines fall, pushed the girl toward it. "You'll have to undress," he told her.

"What?"

"I'm sorry." She really comprehended nothing. He would have to do it for her.

Nelson's voice stopped him. It was suddenly frightened. "I-I'm sick. . . ."

11

Durell and Maj. Miller turned toward him and saw him clutch himself and drop to his knees. They looked at each other helplessly.

Nelson started to say something, but his words were cut off by retching, and Durell heard the growl of vomit as it was ejected from the man's mouth. Durell released the woman and knelt beside him, looking for some way to comfort him. "Take it easy," he said.

The technician at the vital-signs monitor broke in. "Vital signs unstable on Blue Three . . . vital signs unstable!"

The woman started screaming again, her eyes big and crazy.

"We're aware of Blue Three's situation," Durell told the technician. "Discontinue reports." More of that wouldn't help Nelson.

Nelson lay on his side, his body jerking as cramps ripped through his viscera. He was curled in a ball of pain. "Ooohhuuugh! Ow!" The sounds seemed torn from his throat.

Durell looked up at Maj. Miller. The scientist just shook his head.

The woman was quiet again. She stood rigidly, fists tight at her sides, as the helicopter racketed above them, spinning currents of air to batter the deck.

Durell glimpsed the *Henry* beyond the ship's railing, where it rode with its death crew.

A sense of helpless outrage goaded him, but there was nothing to vent it against.

Then he heard a frenzied, sucking sound that was Nelson's death rattle.

After a momentary silence, he rose from Nelson's still form, stood over it briefly, then turned to Maj. Miller. "Let's get in the decontamination capsule; we'll have to put the lady through the shower."

"Bitch," the officer spat.

Durell didn't like that, but he let it pass.

"What about Nelson—Nelson's body?" Maj. Miller asked.

"It'll go to the bottom with the rest." He read his timepiece. A submarine would torpedo both vessels within the hour.

As they entered the decontamination chamber, he gave a glance to Nelson; his eyes roamed darkly over the corpses scattered across the deck. Next time, he thought, the bodies might lie on city streets, mile after mile.

His feelings of urgency and dread were like two hands, choking him. . . .

Chapter 2

"Mr. Durell? I'm Dr. Levin. We've found the bug. I'm supposed to fill you in." He did not offer his hand. He had the red-rimmed, serious eyes of a student and he was K Section's chief of medical research. "Come with me, please," he said.

Durell followed him down a featureless corridor. It was as quiet as a vault. Every room was locked and soundproofed, making for some patients a redoubt, for others a prison. It was where a nuclear physicist from Los Alamos could safely have a nervous collapse. Or a Soviet spy could spill his guts.

Its designation was Building No. 5 at "the Farm," K Section's training and research center in the Maryland countryside. Four hours previously, Durell had arrived there with the sedated woman, since identified as Nydia Duka, a twenty-four-year-old dancer with the New York City Ballet.

"It's a variant *Escherichia coli* bacterium," Dr. Levin said, inserting a plastic card into an electronic scanner. A door popped open. They entered. The still form of Miss Duka lay under smooth sheets, as if dead, beyond the glass wall of an isolation chamber.

"So it was a germ, not a chemical," Durell mused.

"A very special germ. We're calling it *X. coli*. *E. coli* is a common laboratory microbe, used in all sorts of research. Its natural habitat is the gut of human beings and other warm-blooded animals. Normally it doesn't cause any harm. These new bacteria, however—"

"*New*, doctor?"

Dr. Levin looked tired. "They *are* new; they've never been seen before. . . ."

"Are you sure?"

Dr. Levin seemed shocked by the question. "Of course I'm sure. You must have heard of recombinant DNA research. It involves manipulating the characteristics of deoxyribonucleic acid, which is made of molecules that contain the genetic blueprints for all living things. Gene splicing? Genetic engineering?"

"I've heard of it," Durell said.

"That, I have little doubt, is how *X. coli* originated. The chances of it occurring spontaneously, and in the concentrations we have seen, are astronomically high."

Durell's face was grave. "So they're man-made."

"Almost certainly."

"Designed to kill."

"They do it efficiently."

It was almost too horrible to grasp. New life, created in the laboratory as an invisible monster. Durell nodded toward Miss Duka. "But it didn't kill her. Why not?" he asked.

"The answer to that is simple: She's been vaccinated," Dr. Levin said.

"Vaccinated?" Durell stared at the woman, his eyes narrowing. "Then she must have had something to do with what happened to the *Sun Rover*. How long until she wakes up?" he growled.

"It shouldn't be long. Any questions before I go?"

"Yes," Durell said. "If *they* have a vaccine, why can't we get one?"

"We could, given the time," Dr. Levin said. "It's no simple matter. Lots of brilliant work went into *X. coli* and its vaccine, and it can't be reproduced overnight. We'll put everything we've got into trying." He looked gloomy.

Durell regarded the Duka woman thoughtfully. She offered the best hope. For now, the only hope. What if she wouldn't talk? What if he couldn't make her?

As if reading Durell's thoughts, Dr. Levin said, "I don't envy you your job. Those madmen are still loose out there, somewhere, and their weapon is several hundred times more potent a killer than botulism."

The door unlocked behind Durell and a white-garbed attendant entered. The bulge of a revolver showed under his jacket. "Phone, sir." He plugged a jack into the wall and handed Durell a phone without a dial—the Farm was a world unto itself, where outbound calls were discouraged, the simple reason being that every one constituted a potential hole in its massive security dike.

Durell cut his eyes toward Dr. Levin. "I'm leaving," Dr. Levin said.

The man on the other end of the line was General Dickinson McFee, the small, gray chief of K Section. "We've had developments, Samuel," he said. "We've received a note, but it may not be as important as something else. We've learned that a certain Dr. Peter Plettner has been missing for six days. He's a microbiologist. A Nobel prize winner." A touch of excitement hushed McFee's normally reserved voice to a whisper. "His home and laboratory are in Puerto Rico, Samuel."

"Then he could be our man," Durell said.

"Or he could have been kidnapped and his work used by others. We know he's been working in genetic engineering for a Geneva pharmaceutical company, Caske, S.A. Either way, his trail is the one to follow for now." McFee took a breath. Durell envisioned his boss attired in his habitual gray suit, seated straight-backed behind his desk in the innocuous-looking building at No. 20 Annapolis Street. Close at hand would be his diabolical blackthorn walking stick with its poison dart, concealed thermite bomb, and other lethal fixtures dreamed up in K Section's lab. "What I want, Samuel"—no one else called Durell that—"is for you and Maj Miller to bring back whatever can be found in Plettner's laboratory about a vaccine. Maj. Miller will pick you up at the farm."

"Yes, sir. You mentioned a note?"

"Yes. Containing the demands."

"What group? I gather Plettner didn't sign it himself."

"Anonymous." There was a pause. "They want a billion dollars. If they don't get it, they say they'll do to New York City what they did to the *Sun Rover*."

Durell maintained a shocked silence.

"Evacuation is impossible. Where would the people go? How could we prevent panic?" McFee's voice turned resigned. "Besides, the note says the germs will be released immediately if we try to alert the people."

"What can we do but pay?" Durell asked. "When's the deadline?"

"No deadline. They'll give us word soon; that's all they said. The devils. They're giving us time to mull over the consequences if we refuse. Time to sweat." McFee groaned. "But we can't pay. The president hasn't got a billion dollars; he can't ask Congress for it. Word would be all over the country within hours; there would be mass hysteria."

"They tell me the woman was vaccinated," Durell said.

"The note refers to that: Miss Duka was used merely to prove the efficacy of their vaccine. She's innocent."

Durell felt a letdown; he'd counted on her to furnish lots of information. Now it might not amount to much. "Has her history been checked?" he asked.

"Our first thought. She's clean, Samuel. They must have lured her away from the crowd and drugged her. The *Sun Rover* spent last night in San Juan harbor."

"All right," Durell said reluctantly, "but what's the point? They're not selling the vaccine."

"In a way, they are," McFee told him. "For our billion they'll exchange the technology and vaccine they've used.

17

They say it's a reasonable price for a major new weapon. Of course, we couldn't use it anyhow; we're signatory to the Biological Weapons Convention. It's just a sauce they hope will make the outrage of murder and extortion go down easier. Meanwhile, they're telling us that if they must start an epidemic, they also can stop it when the money comes—but then it will cost more!''

"I'll get through here as fast as I can," Durell said.

"She may give us something. You'll fly back to Puerto Rico tonight. Maj. Miller will supply particulars. And Samuel . . ."

"Yes, sir?"

"You have Q clearance—anything goes."

Durell waited another half-hour; it was as if the cold wind beyond the sealed window were blowing through him.

He wore a dark blue worsted-wool suit. He might have been mistaken for a stockbroker but for a hard and haunted look about the eyes. It was the eyes that made others step aside. Now they stared at the pretty face lying on the hospital pillow.

"Miss Duka?"

She did not stir. Purple snow blew in the twilight. The clear sky sat on the world like a block of ice, holding the brooding colors of dusk.

The sunny Caribbean came back into his thoughts. He looked at his watch: How many hours had passed? How many were left. . . ?

The *Sun Rover* lay on the bottom now, with all its passengers. All but one.

She'd have to be hidden until it was safe to let out the true story. Which might mean forever.

For now, to her family, to everyone she knew, she was as dead as the others.

He shook her gently. "Miss Duka?"

Her eyes opened, their brown irises glassy; slowly they focused on him and she frowned. Her body stiffened, as if

18

with fright. He hoped she was rational—there was no guarantee.
"Don't be afraid," he told her.

"Where. . . ?" She looked around in confusion.

"In a U.S. government facility near Washington." He
gave her time, as she regarded him dazedly. At least she
wasn't hysterical. "I'm Sam Durell," he said. "I'm not
going to harm you; I'm here to ask you some questions."

She stared at him. "I can't believe this," she said. "Is it a
dream?"

"No. We need your help, Miss Duka."

"Help?" Her eyes went slowly around the room. He saw
that she was trying to piece together what had happened. He
offered her a glass of water; she took it and drained the glass,
then let her head fall back on the pillow. She closed her eyes,
and her hands trembled on the white sheets. She clenched
them together and lay very still. The room was silent as he
watched her. She might have been made of wax. Finally, she
spoke again. "What happened to the ship?"

"It sank."

"The others?"

"All gone. Dead. I'm sorry."

"Shirley? Jill?" Her voice rose. "Mrs. Dodson? Jim. . . ?"

Durell placed a firm but gentle hand on her shoulder.
"Calm down," he said. "Hold on to yourself."

She relaxed; she seemed too full of shock and misery to
weep. "Why didn't I die, too?" she asked.

"Don't you know?" he asked.

"The last thing I remember, people were sick all over the
ship. Shirley and Jill were helping Mrs. Dodson in our
stateroom, then Shirley got sick, and I went to look for
Jim—he was a man I'd met on the cruise. People were
running through the corridors; some had fallen and lay there
praying and moaning. I heard names . . . a jumble of names
. . . people calling . . . so scared . . . called Jim. . . ."

Durell waited.

"He was dead," she said. "I found him. That's the last I
remember. Oh, lord!"

"It's all over now," Durell told her. He gave her another minute. "The doctors tell us you were inoculated," he said.

She blinked unbelievingly. "How. . . ?"

"You remember nothing of it?"

"No." Her tone was emphatic, defensive.

"It could have happened in San Juan."

"Why? Why me?"

"As an example. Your friends were murdered. The people who did it wanted to prove they had a vaccine. You were just lucky they picked you."

"Lucky? Yes, but I don't deserve it; surely many were more deserving than I. . . ."

"That had nothing to do with it—it was pure chance," Durell said. "Tell me about San Juan," he said.

"There's nothing to tell." She swung her feet to the floor. "I want to see my parents."

"They aren't here," he said.

"Then I'm going home."

"I can't allow that."

She glared at him, bewildered.

"The nightmare isn't over, Miss Duka, but we're all in it now. You, me, the whole world."

"What do you mean?" Her voice rose again. "How can you keep me here? What do you want of me?"

"I told you—San Juan. Somebody inoculated you." He tried to sound reasonable. "What are you hiding?"

"What are *you* hiding, making me a prisoner here?"

Her righteous look made him feel tired. "The government," he said, "is trying to hide the fact that a madman or madmen killed over a thousand people this morning and is threatening to do the same to much of our urban population, unless—"

"This is crazy!"

"Unless we pay them a billion dollars." He held her shoulders.

"I can't go home?" Her face showed fear as plainly as a child's.

"To let the public find out what's happening could be devastating. We can't risk turning you loose," he said.

"Is . . . is it really that awful?" She was beginning to comprehend.

"I'm afraid so. Tomorrow all the papers will carry stories about a collision that sank the *Sun Rover* and a Coast Guard cutter. Most of the story will be speculation, and speculation will breed controversy. There may be calls for an investigation—it could end up before a congressional committee." He watched for her reaction. "Can you imagine the chaos if it came out that your friends were killed by a disease that hit them like a bomb? Think of the panic if the public suddenly found out that the whole country is being threatened, and there's no known defense."

"I-I understand. But I'd keep the secret," she cried.

"How long? Remember, you're the only survivor. How long could you keep the secret, hounded by reporters and dragged before one committee after another?"

She turned her face away for a long moment. He didn't press her; he sensed that he had swayed her. She sat quietly, as if trying to read answers in the twilight beyond the window where frost had etched false shatter-streaks. He heard the distant, muted thump of wind gusting against glass. Finally, she turned back to him. There were tears on her cheeks. "We made love," she said. "last night. I met him in the *Parque de Las Palomas*, above the harbor. He'd followed me from the waterfront, but I wasn't scared. I spent the night with him. Maybe he put something in my drink. I-I didn't want to tell you, but I see I have to. His name was Luis Alegra."

Chapter 3

"The joint chiefs think the Russians know," Maj. Miller said.

"Recon satellites?" Durell asked. It was night on Interstate 270. Maj. Miller had picked him up in a black motor-pool Chevrolet; they were headed into Washington.

"NASA says they were in an orbit allowing surveillance of the *Sun Rover* at the right time. There's been a spurt in radio transmission from Cuba to the Soviet Union."

Durell watched the frigid countryside slide through the darkness. Windows made stilettos of light on the frozen ground. "Did they get wind of the note? The mention of a biological weapon?" he wondered.

"Our orders are to assume security's been broken." The major glanced into the rearview mirror. "The Soviets may believe we would add *X. coli* to our arsenal. If they do, they'll try to get it first. It's that simple."

The Russians. That was all he needed, Durell thought. "The Biological Weapons Convention doesn't mean a damned thing to them, does it?" he said.

"Not if we judge by Afghanistan and Cambodia."

The next minutes passed in silence as Maj. Miller followed Connecticut Avenue into the city. "We have a couple of hours until flight time. General McFee wants us to make a call on Bernhard Caske before we leave," he said.

"Of the Caske pharmaceutical company? I thought he'd be in Europe."

"Normally, he is. He happens to be in town on business." Maj. Miller took several sheets of flimsy from his inside jacket pocket—he was dressed in civvies: a houndstooth jacket and dark slacks—and handed them to Durell. "There's the dope on Caske and his relationship with Plettner, the Einstein of microbiology, as they call him. Don't strain your eye. In a word, it's messy as hell."

Durell glanced through the data by the light of his pen flashlight. He saw that Plettner had a long career in academic research, first at Stanford, then at Princeton, before moving into industrial research on an enormous retainer for Caske, S.A. He was forty-two years old; his wife of eight years, twenty-nine-year-old Muncie, held advanced degrees in biochemistry and was his principal laboratory assistant. He lived and worked on an unnamed island off the south coast of Puerto Rico.

Under *comments*, it was noted that Plettner's career was littered with professional casualties—from the days he'd schemed to head his university's biology department to his unblushing politicking for the Nobel prize. He had a reputation for greed, womanizing, and a raging temper fed by a demanding ego.

Caske used him to hype its stock on the premise that genetic engineering was the growth industry of the future, and Plettner was the best mind in the business. The trouble began, according to the information before Durell, when Dr. Plettner failed to produce any breakthroughs, at least nothing commercially exploitable like synthetic insulin. Now Caske was deeply in debt, its overvalued stock teetering, and facing financial peril.

"There must have been lots of pressure on Plettner to produce," Durell said. "Maybe he couldn't take it."

"And ran away?" Maj. Miller asked. They were on Vermont, not far from Thomas Circle.

"He could hide a long time on a billion dollars," Durell replied. He was thoughtful for a moment. "If only we were sure he was behind it."

"How about that Duka bitch?"

"The Duka lady swears it wasn't Plettner. She was shown his photo. I believe her," Durell said flatly.

"Why? She killed Nelson."

"Nelson's death was an accident."

Maj. Miller's leer was yellow in the light of the dash. "Just because you were naked in the shower with her, don't let it impair your judgment—"

"Shut up," Durell snapped.

"Hey, I didn't mean to make you mad." He halted the car beside the curb. "Here we are: Caske's Washington office. He's expecting us."

As they approached the fanlighted doorway of the trim brick townhouse, Maj. Miller said, "You know, if Bernhard Caske loses Dr. Plettner's services, it'll be the end of his company. Plettner's the only hope he has."

Inside was more like a residence than an office, with comfortable rooms expensively furnished. An aide led them into a library where Bernhard Caske waited. He was tall, with just enough bulk around the middle to look substantial; he wore a full beard trimmed short. He had intelligent eyes, an air of command. His face was flushed; he did not look well.

"Gentlemen." He held out his hand. They introduced themselves. Durell felt a formal aloofness. "Perhaps we should get right to the point?" Caske said.

Durell took the lead. "We understand that your associate, Dr. Plettner, is missing. We're searching for him. Maybe you can help us."

"What does the government of the United States want with him?" Caske asked.

"It's a government matter," Durell said.

"Income taxes?"

"Hardly, sir."

"Then what?" Caske's face hardened.

Durell and Maj. Miller exchanged questioning glances. "It's a matter of the vital national interest. I can't tell you more," Durell insisted. There was a silence.

Caske rose from his chair, clipped the end of a long, black Havana and lighted it with a gold lighter. He looked down at Durell, who remained seated. Caske had a bald head that shone like ivory in the soft light. "National interest means Switzerland's interest to me, not that of the United States," he said.

"You want him back as badly as we do," Durell said.

"He won't do me any good in jail," Caske said.

"He may not go to jail. We simply don't know. We have to find him—lives are involved," Durell said.

"It's not my affair," Caske replied sternly. "Besides, if I knew where he was, don't you think I'd already have gone there?"

"We need his recent work," Durell persisted. "Has he sent anything to the company? Notes? Lab reports? Anything?"

"Hah!" Caske's laugh was disconcerting. "That's what the world would like to know, isn't it? What discoveries has the great Dr. Plettner brought forth? They would like to steal them, if they could. Thieves! Pirates!" He poked the smoldering cigar at Durell. "Well, you can tell them this, Mr. Durell: No one—no one!—will see Dr. Plettner's triumphs until they are safely patented and put before the public under a Caske label!"

"The material would be held in strictest confidence," Durell said.

"With your government? It might as well be printed in the newspapers—it would be in no time!" He lowered his voice. "Just tell them the magnificent Dr. Plettner will return soon. Caske, S.A. will remain preeminent in its field."

It was Durell's turn to stand up. Caske seemed to be trying to turn the affair to some sort of commercial advantage, and Durell was having trouble keeping his Cajun temper under control. Yet, he was not free to tell Caske the extent of the horror hanging over them. He didn't trust the man. He gave him a phone number. "If you change your mind, I can be reached through that number," he told him.

Caske looked stubborn. "You won't tell me your secrets, but you want me to tell you mine."

"Forget it," Durell said, turning to Maj. Miller. "There isn't any more time. Let's get out of here."

Chapter 4

On the final approach to Isla Verde International Airport, San Juan Bay and the San José lagoon were voids in a fiery twinkle that was the sprawl of San Juan. A woven pattern of illumination began as a narrow arm at the fortress of El Morro in the Atlantic, spread between bay and lagoon at Santurce, then widened enormously to the east and west. Lights of merchantmen glowed from moorings in San Antonio Channel, as did those of four cruise liners at tourist piers.

Minutes later Durell and Maj. Miller walked amid purring fountains and palm trees in the open-air concourse of the terminal.

Hours ago San Juan police had been notified to hunt for Luis Alegra. They'd been supplied with Miss Duka's description of him, the places they'd gone the night before—everything she'd remembered—although it was unlikely he'd stayed in town, or that Luis Alegra was his real name. At least the description had been helpful: a tall, thin man with green eyes and a scar through his left eyebrow.

27

There was nothing more to be done in San Juan.

The immediate task was to get Maj. Miller into Dr. Plettner's laboratory, overtly or covertly. Legally or illegally. Maybe he'd find the *X. coli* vaccine there, or at least clues to it, while Durell tried to pick up Plettner's spoor.

They rented a green Datsun and drove south on the Las Américas Expressway toward Ponce, Durell at the wheel. As they crossed the Ruta Panoramica on the island's central mountain spine, a rising breeze broke up the predawn rain clouds, and Durell saw the waters of the Caribbean far in front and the Atlantic to the rear. Then the colors of sunrise swam over the east, and the sun flared brilliantly on the horizon.

Maj. Miller snored beside him as they descended the southern slope of the forested, fog-patched mountain toward Salinas.

On arriving at the shore, he turned off, following a back road to a small fishing village of weathered, tin-roofed houses clustered near a white church. There was a small harbor with a few brightly painted fishing boats. The wind roared among coconut palms that grew down to the high-tide line.

They parked next to the church and walked through beach sand to the piers. The sound of breakers came from down the shore. Gulls shrieked. A few children played.

They found an old man working on the engine of a fishing boat; Durell asked him how much he wanted to ferry them to Plettner's island retreat.

"*Mucho dinero*," the old man said, shaking his head. "People have been shot at out there." He picked up a wrench and studied the engine.

Durell looked at Maj. Miller, who rolled his eyes nervously. "You don't mind getting shot at, do you?" he asked.

"Do I have a choice?" the major asked.

"No." Durell turned back to the fisherman. "We'll pay you for the risk you're taking," he said. "You decide how much."

The old fisherman looked pleased, then thoughtful. Then he said, "It will be costly."

28

"How much?"

"Twenty dollars."

"That's a lot," Durell said.

"I won't take a cent less."

Durell nodded. "It's a deal," he said. "What about the shooting you spoke of?"

The weatherbeaten little man shrugged. "They don't like us. They don't like strangers, either. It's a shame." He sighed. "We used to make a little money taking people out there to see the famous man. Now you take your life in your own hands."

"Has anyone been killed?"

The old man shrugged. "I heard they killed a man from Obispo. It's another village up the coast." He put his wrench away. "They say another was killed also. I don't know where he was from."

"But no one you know; you've seen no one killed?"

The old man stood up, straightening his body with slow effort. "The bullets are real, *señor*."

Durell turned his gaze across the shimmering water. Several small islands hung on the horizon as grayish tufts that seemed to float above the bright sea. He noted with discomfort that the day had already grown hot, although shadows of the palms still were long across the sand. "Well, let's go," he said.

The fisherman held out a gnarled hand; Durell placed a twenty dollar bill in it. The man folded it with care and placed it in the pocket of his stained shirt, and they cast off.

The island was some five miles from shore. It took quite a while to reach it, and the sun climbed higher and the heat lay thick on the water. They had had no breakfast, but Durell was not hungry. He ate when he could; he stayed awake for days, if necessary, driving himself mercilessly.

As they drew closer, he judged the island to be about half a mile long by a mile wide. It rose gently to a round hilltop about a hundred feet high, where he caught glimpses of the ruins of an old white-painted plantation house.

The shoreline alternated between mangrove swamps and

rocky juttings of pitted stone. Here and there yellow beaches swept up to palms and jungle. They were approaching from the lee side, so there was no surf, just a low curl of foam that hissed at the sand.

Durell's eyes quickened with interest as he picked out a single strand of footprints along the beach.

They were close in when the first shot spat from the trees.

"What did I tell you?" the fisherman cried.

Another shot ripped splinters from the deckhouse.

The old man yanked the tiller around.

"What are you doing?" Durell demanded.

"You can have your money," the fisherman cried. He was kneeling beside the tiller. He thrust the twenty dollars at Durell.

"You made a bargain," Durell told him, ignoring the money.

"I'm breaking it."

"No you're not." Durell pushed him aside. He saw Maj. Miller flat on his stomach forward of the deckhouse. "I'll take it in," Durell told the old man. "You just stay down."

"You'd better be ready to die."

"I don't intend to die yet. Where can we land?"

The fisherman looked up from the deck. "There's a cove past that headland."

Durell brought the boat back around, its engine chuffing. He felt sweat trickle down his temple. Maj. Miller pointed toward the shore. "Someone's in the trees. Over there," he called.

Durell kept low, squinting into the glare for a glimpse of the gunman. He saw no one. The sun was high and dazzling, its rays raking his face like hot talons. There had been two shots and nothing more, and he didn't know whether to welcome the silence or fear it. He felt unseen eyes drawing a bead on him. He tried to keep down as he brought the boat chugging around the point indicated by the fisherman. It coasted across clear water in a green cove, the shadow of its hull dragging on the coral and sand beneath them.

He jerked his head down as another shot sent a slug thudding into planking.

"Look!" Maj. Miller called. "In the scrub by that pile of rocks."

Durell nodded. He caught movement in there. "Don't expose yourself any more than you have to," he called. "Let's get off this boat. I think I saw reflection on a scope; I don't see how they can miss many more times." He had them coasting up to a pier. There was a bump and he slammed the propeller into reverse, threw his bag over the side and leaped across. "Throw your bag. Jump," he called.

Maj. Miller flew onto the pier, went down on his knees, and grabbed his bag.

"Come on!" Durell darted into the jungle, followed by the major. A bullet cut twigs in his path. He ducked behind a tree, looked back, and saw the fishing boat heading out to sea.

The air was steaming. Insects hummed and buzzed. Wind rattled the foliage.

He heard his blood thumping.

"You circle one way. I'll go the other," he told Maj. Miller.

The pudgy officer nodded.

Durell scrambled up a slope, fighting creepers and brambles, fronds and branches. He took a moment to get his bearings, slapped a mosquito, listening. Sweat stung his eyes. He was tempted to unholster his .38, but reconsidered. No one had been harmed yet, and a gunfight might prove a tragic mistake. He guessed he'd come about the right distance to circle behind his quarry. He turned toward the sea, placing each step silently. Spears of sunlight fell through the treetops; spongy humus gave way to stone underfoot. He could see patches of sky through the jungle ahead, indicating he had returned almost to the water's edge.

"Stop right there, mister."

The words came from his rear, and he felt the muzzle of a rifle in his back. The voice was a woman's.

"Put the gun down. Can't we talk?" he said.

31

"There's no need for talk; you're going straight back where you came from."

"The boat's gone."

"Then I hope you like to swim. March." She poked him with the gun.

He spun, used his elbow to knock the muzzle aside, and easily twisted the weapon from her grasp, throwing her backwards. He was surprised to find himself holding a collector's gun, a beautifully chased Weatherby .300 Magnum Mark V with a carved stock. The woman was dressed in jeans and a simple print blouse; long, rippled hair the colors of chestnut and mahogany framed a face that, behind its rage, had the round, regular features of a midwestern cheerleader. She had fallen and glared at him with iridescent blue eyes. She lunged, hissing with fury, swinging a heavy rock at his face. He threw the rifle aside and grabbed her; it went off.

"Sam! You all right?" Maj. Miller called.

"We're over here," Durell shouted. Deftly, he spun the woman and pinned her arms to her sides. She was small and light and nicely curved. She kicked his shins and tried to sink her claws into him.

"Let me go!" she cried.

"Okay, when you'll listen and stop trying to brain me." He tightened his grip. A pinched cry of pain caught in her throat. "I don't like hurting you," he told her. "Who are you?" His information was that there were two women on the island: Mrs. Muncie Plettner and Mrs. Tina Durso. Mrs. Durso was the nineteen-year-old wife of Dr. Plettner's secretary, Ronald Durso. Durell took a guess. "Mrs. Durso?"

"What? No, you gorilla!" She seemed further angered, as if insulted—he surmised she didn't care much for the Durso woman. "Muncie Plettner, then?" he said.

"What's it to you?"

"I'm Sam Durell. I'm here on government business."

"You're trespassing." Her teeth found his arm and sank into the muscle. Pain and anger flashed through him; he threw her away, and she hit the ground hard, the breath knocked out

32

of her. She looked dazed and shocked. He yanked her up and shook her so hard her hair fell across her face.

Maj. Miller came crashing through the undergrowth, panting and red in the face. He stopped wide-eyed, hands on his hips. "I might have known," he said angrily. "A woman."

"It's Mrs. Plettner," Durell said. Continuing to hold her by the shoulders, he told her, "That's Maj. Miller. We're here to help you. Why don't you cooperate?"

"Fat chance. Give me my rifle."

"I'm sorry. What are you afraid of?"

"I don't want you here. I want to be left alone," she shouted.

"We're staying the night," he said, trying to keep his voice calm. "Then you can have your wish. We know your husband is missing; we've got to find him."

"This isn't the place to look," she said.

"It'll have to do for a start—unless you can tell us where to go."

"I'll tell you where to go: Go to hell." She stared at him defiantly. She was not struggling anymore. He returned her gaze steadily, and she faltered. She lifted her eyes back to him; this time there was something haunted in them. "Listen," she said, "six years ago, this place was a paradise. People left us alone. Peter could do his work. Then—then he won the prize. It nearly ruined our lives. Hordes of people just descended on us. Reporters, university presidents, advertising executives . . . cranks, crackpots, students. . . . Peter's work dried up. Don't you see?"

"I see." Durell nodded. "You can't go killing people, though."

"I didn't kill anybody."

"That's not the word out."

She studied him for a second. Her blue eyes had a smoky look in the leafy shadows. "What *is* the word on me, Mr. Durell?"

"Beware," he said shortly. "Show us to your house; tell us about your husband."

"I don't seem to have much choice," she said.

33

He released her, and she turned and walked into the surrounding wall of foliage.

"What about this?" It was Maj. Miller, showing him the Weatherby.

"Bring it," he said, "but let's keep it out of her reach until she cools off." He followed her into the jungle.

It was apparent that Mrs. Plettner knew the island well, because she followed a path—if you could call it that—that he couldn't see. They didn't go inland, as he'd expected they would; they went along the shore, where the blue of the ocean was often visible through the trees. It took about ten minutes to reach the house. He became aware of it as an irregular shape of yellow stone that materialized in glimpses through the leaves. He thought it certainly offered privacy—perhaps isolation was a better word. Mrs. Plettner showed them inside, where he found impressive glass walls with a view of rolling surf and windblown palms. The furnishings were contemporary and expensive, with such touches as a collection of French art glass that showed a willingness to spend on a rich man's scale.

Mrs. Plettner sent her handyman Phineas to retrieve the valises that Durell and Maj. Miller had left on the pier, and called on a maid named Joanna to fetch coffee, for which Durell was thankful. The woman was no longer overtly hostile, and Durell had some reason to hope she had worked matters through to a proper conclusion. Maybe she'd come to accept the need for his help—if she were ever to know what had become of her husband—even if she resented having the help forced on her.

"Here comes Ron," she said. She didn't sound pleased. "He's Dr. Plettner's secretary and business manager—but I suppose you already know that."

Durell made no reply.

With a curl of her lip, she said, "He has a little bitch of a wife. You'd better watch out for her." She gave him a look that admitted his attractiveness.

"That makes two of you to look out for," he told her.

"Yes, but not for the same reason," she retorted.

34

He heard the door close and turned to meet the questioning face of Durso. He was a tall man with hard, thin lips and ambitious eyes. "Guests, Muncie?" he asked, raising a black eyebrow. He wore white slacks and a short-sleeved shirt and tie, no jacket.

"Not exactly. In fact, I'm their prisoner," she told him as the maid brought in the coffee. She sounded only half joking, but Durso refused to take her seriously.

"You're treating your captors with plenty of hospitality," he said. "May I have a cup, too?" The maid had left the urn and he helped himself.

"The big one beat me up," Mrs. Plettner said. "He thinks I'm the wild woman of Borneo. His name is Sam Durell. The other one is Maj. Miller."

Durso offered his hand, and started to introduce himself. "I'm Ronald Durso, Dr. Plettner's—"

"Oh, they know all about you. They were sent by the government, and they know everything there is to know," Mrs. Plettner interrupted.

"I wish we did," Durell told him.

"Why the rifle?" Durso asked him.

"We were forced to disarm Mrs. Plettner," Durell said.

"I forced him!" she snapped. "As if he didn't force his way onto my island!"

Durso chose to treat the matter lightly, but Durell didn't trust his smile—it might have shielded anything. "Muncie seems to feel we're under seige, especially since Dr. Plettner disappeared so mysteriously," he said.

"Our aim is to find him," Durell said.

"We'd be grateful."

"Without Dr. Plettner the Caske company hasn't much to offer its stockholders, has it," Durell pointed out. "You're salaried by Caske and not Dr. Plettner, aren't you?"

Durso sipped his coffee and nodded. "The arrangement saved him the expense and bother of hiring someone."

"It also made sure that Caske would have its loyal representative in Plettner's camp, watching him, maybe prodding him a bit?" Durell said.

"What are you getting at?" Durso studied Durell for a suspicious moment, his black eyes flickering.

"I just wish I knew how much pressure Dr. Plettner was under," Durell told him.

Durso lowered his coffee cup. "I can assure you I've had only Dr. Plettner's best interest at heart. I was the one who reported his disappearance to the police."

"Like a fool," Mrs. Plettner said.

"Muncie seems to take her husband's absence without much worry," Durso remarked. He chuckled without mirth.

"Of course I'm worried, but I told you he'd be back; he always comes back."

"Muncie!" Durso's tone seemed to carry a warning not to reveal more.

Durell ignored it. "What do you mean, he always comes back?" he asked.

She let a couple of seconds pass. Durell sipped his coffee and waited, watching her as combers exploded in the background. She glanced at Durso, then back to Durell. "He's gone away before," she said.

"But this time . . ." Durso began.

"This time he's been gone longer. So what?" she said. She sounded impatient with Durso's caution. "You just never reported him missing. Now the police are all stirred up; if it doesn't get into the papers, it'll be a miracle. Peter will be humiliated when he comes home."

There came another woman's voice, redolent with a plush southern accent, reasoning as if talking to a child. "Muncie, honey, we couldn't just ignore that he was gone, not after a whole week."

"I'm sure you'd notice, Tina," Muncie replied. The words slipped from between her lips like ice cubes.

The woman entering the room wasn't likely to be ignored either, Durell decided. She was a Celtic beauty with the flawlessly white skin that adorns some redheads—she seemed to have spent as much effort avoiding the tropical sun as her deeply tanned husband had exercised in soaking it up. His quick guess was that she resented being stuck here; the glance of her green eyes told him she was glad to have visitors. She wore shorts and a halter top, showing off a slender, well-proportioned figure that was more girlish than Mrs. Plettner's. She chewed gum, which her husband appeared not to approve of; he gave her a look, and she took it out of her mouth. Durell saw her slyly drop it into a potted plant.

Muncie spoke in a cynical purr. "Well, Sam Durell and Maj. Miller, here you have us all: the missing scientist's wife; his ever-so-dedicated secretary; and, completing the fiasco, Mrs. Tina Durso, the 'other woman' . . .''

"Now, see here—'' Tina began.

Muncie brushed it aside. ". . . who was discovered fairy-tale fashion working in a Miami delicatessen by his lordship over there." She pointed at Durso, who scowled. "Ron likes them young and pretty, don't you, dear?'' she needled. "Despite the difference in their ages, he doesn't deserve much credit for sweeping the girl off her feet—she's shown she'll fall on her back at the slightest push."

"You don't have any right to say that!'' Tina cried. "What'll these people think? You're jealous—you're just insanely jealous because I'm younger and prettier . . . just because you never could make Peter happy!''

"Not the way you could, you—''

"Stop it!'' It was Durso, his lips tight with anger. He gave Durell and Maj. Miller an embarrassed glance. "You apologize!'' he told Muncie.

"Not much chance of that, kiddo,'' she answered. She seemed almost amused by the furor she had caused.

Durso's face turned the color of a biscuit, and he and Muncie stared at each other with stubborn dislike.

"I don't need her apology; she's no lady,'' Tina said. "Excuse me, gentlemen.'' She turned and strode out of the room.

Maj. Miller snorted discreetly and cut his eyes toward Durell, as if to say the scene justified his contempt for women.

Muncie seemed to have caught the glance. "Aren't we a nice little family?'' she said.

"I didn't come here to referee a feud or judge anyone's private life," Durell told her.

"No one asked you to come here at all," she reminded him.

Durell was wary of her; she was too bitter for her own good—or anyone else's. She'd made it obvious that she believed Durso's young wife had been having an affair with her husband. She was jealous, and jealousy made her even more dangerous.

He dismissed Tina as an adolescent sexpot who'd found security and status with Durso, but hadn't had enough sense to let well enough alone when it came to the famous Dr. Plettner. Life on the island probably had been boring, in spite of occasional hops to Paris or London as part of an international celebrity's entourage. Or had Durso left her here, hidden away, so she couldn't embarrass him? That might fit, Durell thought. Durso looked like the type who would jettison anyone if it suited his ambition.

As these thoughts sped through Durell's mind, Muncie lighted a cigarette, blew smoke at the ceiling. Then she said, "Well, as long as you're here, what about my husband? What's the government interested in him for? It isn't as if he made atomic bombs, you know."

"It almost could be," he said.

"Are you talking about the genetic experiments?" She and Durso exchanged amused glances. For once they smiled at the same time. "Such overblown nonsense," she said.

"Really," Durso seconded.

"It isn't for me to decide," Durell said. He wished he were free to tell all he knew—*then* let them call it nonsense. But the secret of the hideous threat hanging over them had to stay with him and Maj. Miller. All he was allowed to say was, "We consider your husband a national asset and we're concerned for his safety."

"But he works for a Swiss company."

"True, but his disappearance made waves clear to the White House."

"Are you trying to intimidate me? It won't do you any

good. I'm not scared of the White House." She puffed her cigarette and blew smoke from between round red lips.

Maj. Miller spoke up. "Why should you feel intimidated, Mrs. Plettner? Surely your interests coincide with ours. Don't you want your husband back?"

"Did anybody say I didn't?"

Durso said, "Believe me, Major, we're delighted to have the government's help in finding Dr. Plettner."

"Hi-ho"—Muncie lifted her coffee in a toast—"old mealy-mouth rides again. Of course you're happy—without Peter, you'd be nothing."

Durell saw Durso's jaw tightening angrily. "Why are you so damned determined to be unpleasant and uncooperative?" he demanded. "Damned if it doesn't make me wonder . . ." He hesitated.

"What?" she asked. "What do you wonder?"

"It makes me wonder if—if you didn't have something to do with—with whatever happened to him!"

"So!" Her laugh was bitter. "I'm the prime suspect now?"

"We've seen your jealousy," Durso said. "Even they have." He indicated Durell and Maj. Miller.

Durell spoke up. "We don't know what's happened to Dr. Plettner; it's a bit early for accusations. Let's talk sensibly. Mrs. Plettner, when was the last time you saw your husband?"

She made a face, as if resigning herself to being questioned. "Thursday night, just before bedtime," she said.

"*Before* bedtime?"

"We don't sleep together," she said frankly. "I kicked him out of my bed when I found out about Tina."

"You found out nothing!" Durso snapped.

The sarcastic smile that seemed to be her trademark returned. "You blind fool," she told him.

"Break it up," Durell commanded.

"Men are so stupid," Muncie said.

"You're going to have a real murder on your hands if she doesn't shut up about my wife," Durso told Durell.

Muncie said, "The proper thing for you to do is get out of my house and my life. And take that little . . . your wife with you." She turned to Durell. "I'd fire him, if I could. He won't quit; he'll take any abuse to stay on. Caske must pay him a pretty penny. Am I right, Ron?"

"Of course," Durso said. "Not that it's any of your business." He gave a disparaging snort. "While we're at it, where would you be without Dr. Plettner?"

"Better ask where he'd be without me! I worked side by side with him for nothing!" She turned sullen blue eyes on the floor. "Now he's throwing it all away. He's turned into a lush, Mr. Durell."

"Muncie!" It was Durso, as if he would have stopped her but was too late. He turned to Durell. "All right, Dr. Plettner has a drinking problem—but this mustn't go any further; it could ruin his reputation and the company's financial position. In any case, he isn't just off on some toot, I just know it. . . ."

Durell stared at them. Maybe Plettner's drinking explained Muncie's bitterness more than his dalliance with the likes of Tina. Alcoholism destroyed dreams as well as people.

If a man were on the skids, it also could explain a mad, desperate act. . . .

Muncie's voice had lost its bite for a change. There was a plea for understanding in it now. "Peter is a child in so many ways," she said. "That's why he's temperamental. He's really scared, scared of failure. The demands, the expectations— they were too much. He'd been struggling for years when the Caske company came along and practically handed him a fortune. Who could have resisted taking it? But then the company made such a big deal of it, as if he were going to solve the greatest genetic mysteries by noon the next day." She took a discouraged breath. "So what happened? You know if you'd bought Caske stock two or three years ago. It didn't just double or triple in value, it increased fivefold, then tenfold—in twenty-one months! But the lab doesn't work like the stock market. Everything is painstaking; it takes time." Her laugh was gloomy. "You should have seen Mr. Caske himself flying in, falling on his knees. 'Where is it, my boy? Where is it? Where is the miracle!' So Peter began rushing things, and he came up with a goodie or two—and some baddies. The stock started slipping; last week it'd lost three-quarters of the appreciation that had made millionaires of everyone the year before. And who's getting all the blame? Take a guess." She ground out the stub of her cigarette.

"Well, you know what they say, Mr. Durell: You can't run away from your troubles. Peter doesn't believe that. I've always found him when he's tried, though, and more often than not he comes home with his tail between his legs. I send his freeloading pals packing, pay off his whores. . . ." She stopped and shook her head. "But why am I telling you all this?" she wondered.

"I hope you've told it to the police," he said.

She nodded. "They've scoured every dive from San Juan to Mayagüez."

"Mrs. Plettner . . . could his disappearance be more serious than you think?" he asked.

She seemed abruptly uncertain, as if what she'd said had been a bluff and the bluff were crumbling. "Do . . . do you think something really may have happened to him?" she asked.

"I don't know," Durell said. He took her hand. It was cold. "You were his lab assistant. Will you accompany Maj. Miller to Washington to talk to some people? It's vitally important that we find out what Dr. Plettner was working on." She looked bewildered. He forestalled her question. "I can't tell you why, but it's of great concern."

Durso interrupted. "I'm afraid that would be impossible, Mr. Durell—not that we don't wish to cooperate to the fullest, but our hands are tied, legally. Whatever Mrs. Plettner knows of Dr. Plettner's work—her knowledge—is Caske property. It's a trade secret. Can't have the government privy to it. Why, that would put it into the public domain."

"We'd respect your trade secrets," Durell told him. "Mrs. Plettner. . . ?"

"If it's all that important, I wish I could help, but I can't," she said. "Honest, I don't know anything Peter's been up to for the last ten weeks. He locked me out of his lab."

"Did he say why?"

"We . . . we were having marital problems, as I've told you. He just told me he preferred working alone. I thought that was why. I didn't ask." She shook her head. "I didn't want to fight over it," she said.

Durell saw no point in fretting over what was done. "Look," he said, "my superiors want Maj. Miller to go through the laboratory, check out your husband's work in progress and his notes. . . ."

Again Durso blocked the way. "Nobody can go into Dr. Plettner's laboratory without his or the company's express permission. I'm sorry, Mr. Durell."

Durell turned to Muncie once more. "I'm not sure of the legal technicalities," she told him. "I don't want to cause trouble for Peter when he comes back. . . ."

"I have to insist," Durell said.

She looked at Durso questioningly. In spite of their mutual dislike, they were bound together by their ties to Dr. Plettner. Durso said, "And we have to refuse you. You have no legal right to force us. It's private property. Besides, most items of interest will be flown to Geneva tomorrow, so you'd hardly—"

"Geneva?" Durell was taken aback.

"Company headquarters. A charter jet's coming in the morning." Durso lifted a black eyebrow. "We can't have everything left lying about, can we? Dr. Plettner may return, but what if he doesn't? The matter involves company secrets, patents—your own Supreme Court ruled that newly created life forms could be patented. Much better that we tuck all the information safely away for the time being."

Durell exchanged looks with Maj. Miller. It was clear that the only thing left to do was bide their time until they could break into the lab. Maj. Miller would have to spend a busy night there.

Further persistence for permission might only create more obstacles.

"Looks like we've struck out," he told Muncie.

"Serves you right," she said. Her animosity didn't hold

the enthusiasm it had earlier. She'd begun to look deeply worried.

"Put us up for the night?"

"Since you're asking, instead of demanding," she assented. "We'll arrange transportation back to the mainland for you in the morning."

The maid showed them to their rooms. Durell put his burdens aside and fell into a deep sleep. . . .

Chapter 5

"There's lots of anger floating around here, Sam," Maj. Miller said.

"The question is whether it has anything to do with the matter at hand," Durell replied.

"People do strange things under pressure. They can go wacko," the major said.

Durell considered it again, as he had a hundred times before. Whoever was responsible for what had happened on the *Sun Rover* certainly was insane—which meant that the processes of his mind took place in a dark region beyond the logic of rational men. You couldn't know what would come next. Which meant you were, to some degree, at his mercy.

He suppressed a shudder, glad to be out of Plettner's house for a stroll and a dip.

He had slept several hours, taking the chance to catch up on badly needed rest. Awakening in his air-conditioned bedroom, he'd felt chilled and groggy, fretful over a fuzz of dream memories tangled in his imagination. The fresh air revived him, hot and damp as it was even at the final hour of daylight, and the cries of birds and insects seemed to tune his senses back to reality.

Maj. Miller persisted, his tone speculative. "You know, Sam, it's possible that Mrs. Plettner *did* kill her husband—all the easier to believe for the way she handled that rifle—but what hasn't been said is that Ronald Durso could have done him in as well. It seems to me that he should've been as jealous as Mrs. Plettner, if not more so." Maj. Miller, staring across the water, combed his blowing hair with his fingers.

"Jealousy wouldn't account for the scheme against the government," Durell said. "Somebody—and Dr. Plettner seems most likely the one—put the *X. coli* thing together to get money. Who's sleeping with whom doesn't seem to matter. I don't think either of them killed him."

"You're assuming he developed the *X. coli*," Maj. Miller argued. "Even if he did, there's the possibility that someone else got hold of it. If that happened, he could be dead."

They stood at the edge of a lagoon, a broad jade field shot with amber lights.

Durell waded in and swam without being able to wash a sense of foreboding and frustration from his mind. He'd dreamed of the ship, the corpses, the horrible death of Nelson. . . .

The pain of the dream had been real, but how insignificant it all was compared to what might come. . . .

Durell crossed the lagoon twice, slicing through the glassy water with easy power, relishing the deep, clean breaths that filled his lungs. By the time he stood dripping and gleaming on the warm sand, he'd pushed the horror away from his thoughts once more.

Maj. Miller toweled his round belly. "I've got to get into that lab, Sam. When are you going to help me?"

"I've been waiting for dark. I'll get you in," Durell told him. He wiped salt water from his eyes. The sun seemed to pause on the rim of the ocean, then plunged from sight. A great flare of orange incandescence flamed toward the heavens, deepened to vermilion, and slid in a golden avalanche below the horizon. The world turned indigo.

Maj. Miller said, "The sooner the better. I'll have to look through the lab notes and try to sort out the stuff I find. It may take me most of the night."

"Just be careful," Durell said.

"I doubt there are any *X. coli* in there," Maj. Miller replied. "What I really hope is that I'll find a clue to Dr. Plettner's vaccine. Maybe it'll give a head start to our boys back in Washington."

"Still, if that's the lab where *X. coli* was created . . ."

"I don't suppose there's a deadly organism known to man that I haven't worked with."

"Under proper laboratory safeguards," Durell pointed out. "And you can barely say this bug *is* known to man."

"I'm not worried. Besides, we can't leave everything to you. But, listen"—Maj. Miller touched his arm—"once I go into the lab, don't open the door again, just to be on the safe side. You'll know everything is okay when I come back out."

Durell saw that Maj. Miller was more concerned than he cared to admit. "And what if you don't come back?" he asked.

"It's a mighty impressive house to have to burn down. It would serve that vixen right, though," the major replied, making light of Durell's worry. His face was serious, however, as he added, "That's what has to be done if anything goes wrong. There won't be any saving me, you understand? Torch it."

Durell spoke in a flat voice. "I understand. Let's get back to the house. When you're dressed, come to my room and wait."

The breeze had freshened. He heard the thunder of surf from the other side of the island, amid the clash of fronds and the rubbing of branches. Far to the east the tower of a storm cloud blotted out the white glitter of countless stars.

One of Plettner's watchdogs barked. The sound was dim and fragile in the wind.

Durell felt jumpy, but he didn't share his edginess with Maj. Miller. It was nothing concrete, anyhow, just something in the air, a premonition that teased the back of his neck with icy fingers.

It whispered of death.

Seen through staggering trees, cheerful lights shone from the house, as if to mock his instincts.

Again in his room he showered away the salt and donned a tropical-weight suit of gun-metal blue. Under the jacket he fastened a shoulder holster with the familiar weight of his snub-nosed .38 in it.

His room opened onto a poorly lit corridor, leading past sliding glass doors through which he saw the inky shapes of trees blown by the wind. He continued on to a plain locked door at the end of the corridor, picked the lock, and pushed through into darkness. A stillness to the air told him this was a small room; his hand touched a lamp, found the switch. He was in an office of some sort. A simple metal desk was stacked with ledgers and bills; tape coiled from an adding machine. He killed the light, exiting into a large bedroom dark enough so that the flicker of lightning from the distant squall played back from satin covers on a king-size bed. Going to the first of two doors, he found a capacious bathing-dressing area; the second door took him into a short, T-shaped space where another door held the label DANGER: DO NOT ENTER. The door had a window about the size of his hand, but the room was dark, and he couldn't see anything through it.

He bent and examined the lock, looked cautiously around, and went to work. A few seconds later the door swung in to reveal a shadowed interior with long workbenches, glass cabinets, stainless steel machinery, and sophisticated electronic gear. It could only have been Dr. Plettner's laboratory.

He quietly snapped the door shut, making sure it remained unlocked.

"Hi." It was Tina.

"Hello," he replied casually, hoping she hadn't seen him close the door. "Why the flashlight?" he asked.

"I was going to look outside. I was getting dressed, and I heard something. Was it you?"

"I haven't been outside," he said. He regarded her with a quick sweep of his dark eyes. The low lighting rested on her clear skin like the icing on a cake. Her face held an open, childlike frankness beneath its billowing cloud of fine red hair. Her makeup was fresh, and she'd changed into a short yellow skirt. A clinging tank top showed the nipples of her breasts as little buttons under the cloth.

The watchdog barked, and she took a quick step closer. "Something's out there," she said.

"Go back to your room. I'll see about it," he said. "Dogs bark at anything when the wind's blowing."

"Can I stay with you? Just a little while?" She gave him a pleading look.

"I don't think your husband would like that. Where is he?"

"I don't know. In his study, I guess. It's his hideout."

Durell cocked an ear to the outdoors; the wind roared and howled, whined and hissed. "What does a man like him have to hide from?" he asked.

"Me." She looked shamefaced, then helpless. "I'm not very good company for a man with his brains."

"He married you, didn't he?"

"Yes, but . . ." She hesitated. "I think he sees it's a mistake." She became secretive. "He never even introduced me to his family, you know. Oh, I don't want to meet them—I wouldn't know how to act. Honest."

"Are you always so hard on yourself?"

"Not always . . . I know I'm pretty." She gave him a sly smile. "Don't you think?"

"You're very attractive," he said.

"Oh, attractive. I like that word. It's got class." She came a step closer.

"What does Dr. Plettner think of you?" Durell asked.

"He's sweet, at least. He never tries to put me down."

Durell waited, but she added nothing. "Did he ever seem deranged? Crazy?" he asked.

She looked shocked by such a question. "Heavens, no! I mean, he definitely isn't any ordinary kind of man. And he—well, he likes the juice. I don't hold that against him, not with what he has to live with. I mean Muncie . . . Muncie . . ." Tina worked at forming her thoughts. "Muncie was the sort of girl meant to go up the ladder with her man. But if he slipped, she didn't know how to handle it. It was like she had her eyes on the stars, and when she had to look down, she just couldn't. I'm not going to say anything bad about her. I guess it's just that, well, coming from a long line of sharecroppers, I know all about hard times. . . ."

"So Dr. Plettner began turning to you," Durell suggested.

"Yes." She looked him straight in the eye. "Well, what if he did? I may not be much in the brains department, but Ron always said there was one thing I could do very well."

"And what was that?"

"Do I have to spell it out for you? My goodness. You know: s-e-x?"

"You feel that's all you have to offer?"

"What do you mean 'all'?" she flared. Then, abashed, she added, "Well, I don't feel that way with Peter. I—I suppose that's what made me love him," she said defiantly.

"What about your husband?" Durell asked.

She shrugged her inviting white shoulders. "As long as Peter and I don't flaunt ourselves, it isn't hard to keep Ron happy," she said. "He only married me because he wanted a woman in his bed when he was stuck on this godforsaken island. I knew that. I didn't object. Look, it's a big step up from carving salami."

Durell thought about the two men sharing this luscious child. The arrangement seemed to have been casual, with only Muncie objecting. Durso didn't like for Muncie to make a fuss about it; he'd seen that. But it could have worked to Durso's advantage—if he'd been using his wife to ingratiate himself further with Plettner. There were other possibilities. Maybe Durso had hated it, but hadn't dared to interfere. Or maybe he'd got rid of Plettner in a jealous rage, then, recognizing the possibilities, had stolen the *X. coli* and engineered the *Sun Rover* disaster. He'd told Durell he was glad to have the government looking for Plettner, but that really meant nothing. He'd bear watching.

"Maybe," Durell told Tina, "you only thought Ron was content with your . . . arrangement."

A red fingernail drew a circle on his chest. "Honey," she said, "I'll bet I know more about what makes guys like him tick than you'll ever know." She had another thought. "No, it was Dr. Plettner who was unhappy, not Ron. Peter was born to be unhappy, I think."

Durell realized how much time must have passed. Maj. Miller would be waiting. "You'd better go," he told Tina.

She looked a little surprised. "Alone?" she asked.

"Leave me your flashlight," he said.

"Was that the dog again?" she asked.

"I think so. I'll have a look outside," he said.

"Would you? I'd feel ever so much safer." Her green eyes were appreciative.

She seemed in no rush. "I like you," she told him with her usual frankness. "I'm lonely, and I hate this island. Maybe later, we could . . . talk some more? Do you like swimming by moonlight?"

"There is no moon," Durell said. "Goodbye."

She waggled her fingers goodbye. "Don't miss cocktails," she said as she walked away. High wedge-soled shoes shaped her legs to perfection.

When she had closed a door behind her, Durell returned to his room the same way he had come.

"Did you fix it so I could get into the lab?" the major asked.

Durell nodded. "They're having cocktails. Now's your chance. I'll make an excuse for your absence."

"Roger." Maj. Miller paused at the door and looked back. "Look out for those women, both of them. Couple of over-wrought females. They don't play by the rules, you know."

"Who does?" Durell asked.

The major smiled and left.

Durell rubbed his nose, waiting as seconds passed. Then

he slipped into the windswept, jasmine-scented night. The air felt thick and warm and laden with the dusky vapors of vegetation. Its fragrance was touched by the smell of distant rain, the tang of iodine from the ocean. The thunderhead seen earlier had blown far to the west, and the sky was a sparkling sheet of stars with the Milky Way hanging low. The lights of Ponce showed as a vague blush on the western horizon. Normally he would have used the flashlight, but something told him not to. He had shared Tina's concern, had heard or felt something dangerous, like the presence of an intruder. There had been nothing objective to base it on, if you didn't count the bark of a dog on a windy night. But he had learned to give tremors of instinct due notice; they had saved his life on more than one occasion.

He went in a silent crouch along the wall of the house, taking care to bend below shafts of light beaming out of windows. After ten steps, he stopped, listened. The dog hadn't barked for some time.

Brush and trees made a surrounding wall that heaved and roared under the mauling of the wind. He could make out nothing in there, so he took another ten steps, then another.

His toe caught on something. A steel chain—the dog's chain. But where was the dog?

He followed the chain with rising apprehension. The animal lay a few feet away, its head thrown back unnaturally.

It was dead.

Dead of a broken neck.

Chapter 6

Durell drew his pistol and flattened himself amid the stones.

Someone had to be out there, and his eyes strained to pick him out. Whoever it was seemed to be playing a waiting hand, maybe in hopes of making a move after everyone was asleep. By killing the dog they had effectively silenced the alarm. They'd probably cut the phone line as well.

He chewed his lip and let time flow with the patience of a hunter.

He could see nothing in the tangle of leaves and vines that made a screen a few yards from his face. He heard, or felt, the beating of his heart despite the bedlam of the wind. Optimistically, no one had seemed to see him either.

He wriggled around and wormed his way back along the foundation until he found the door from which he had exited. He slid back inside, turning the latch behind him. His face gleamed with beads of sweat. Stone-colored smears of dust blotched his suit.

He found Durso, Tina, and Muncie in the enormous

cathedral-ceilinged living area having drinks and chatting as if they were the best of friends. It made him think he must have been the catalyst for all the bitterness that had come out earlier. Left alone, they'd glossed it over again, accommodating each other like the lonely castaways they literally almost were.

Despite the cool air-conditioning, Muncie had laid a fire in the coral and stone fireplace, where she burned eroded sticks of driftwood that looked like bones. She had left her jeans behind, and was stunning in a full-cut lounging outfit of navy blue watered-silk slacks and a top with a gold sash. She'd pulled the autumn-brown strands of her hair back severely and twisted them into a tight bun at the nape of her slender neck. Durso was there in a white jacket and open-necked shirt, a highball in his hand. Durell wondered if Tina had shared her fears of intruders with him. Tina was perched on the raised hearth, blithely sipping a drink. He'd have thought nothing had disturbed her simple mind, had he not known better.

He hated to spoil such a picture of conviviality, even if it were rank with hypocrisy.

Without any preliminaries, he turned to Muncie. "I have some bad news, but I want you to stay calm," he said. "Someone killed your watchdog." She sucked in her breath and looked at the others. "Whoever did it must still be out there," he said. "They may hope to take us by surprise, maybe after we've gone to bed."

She stared at him, going pale.

Tina said, "I knew it. I knew someone was sneaking around out there."

Muncie found her voice. "What do you mean, 'take us by surprise?' You really think people are . . . are still lurking out there?"

"My government may not be the only one after Dr. Plettner's material," he said, his tone grim.

"Who else is?"

"As I told you before, there are things I can't talk about,

but you're right in the middle of a vicious little war, and you'd better believe it."

"What are we going to do? I don't know anything about fighting wars." Her eyes went to Durso and Tina.

Durso said, "We've got to get off this island, that's for sure. Do it now is my suggestion."

"But our plane isn't due until six in the morning. There's no other way tonight," Muncie said.

"Don't be silly. Call the air taxi out of Ponce; we'll arrange to be picked up there for Geneva," Durso replied. He tossed down the last of his highball. "I'll go to the lab and finish the packing."

"Wait," Durell called. Maj. Miller would be in the lab. Durso had to be kept away, but he didn't think that would be too difficult. "You may as well save the effort," he told him. "There's no way to get in touch with the air taxi. Try the phone."

Durso gave him a look of disbelief, picked up the phone, joggled the button. Warily, he replaced it in its cradle. "No dial tone," he said.

"So I guessed," Durell said. "The phone lines have been cut. We're stuck here until morning, whatever happens."

They stared at him with stricken expressions. Durso looked like a cornered fox. The wind moaned against the glass wall that faced the ocean. Through reflections of fire and lamps, Durell could see the phosphoresence of curling breakers.

His voice was taut. "Where do you keep your guns?" he asked.

"You have the Weatherby, or Maj. Miller does," Muncie said. Then, with alarm, "Where's Maj. Miller?"

"He's resting," Durell replied. "The trip tired him more than he thought. The guns?" he asked.

"In a cabinet in the library, through there." She pointed.

"Where's your handyman?"

"In the servants' wing. What—?"

"Get him in here, and the maid, too. We want everybody with a finger to pull a trigger."

Durell hurried toward the library, which was in the vicinity

54

of the laboratory. Durso was a worry, because he had followed, and might take it in his mind to check there. They found the gun case, which held two rifles, a .22 semiautomatic and a bolt-action .30-06, and two shotguns, a 12-gauge and a 16-gauge. In a drawer was a fancy, long-barreled .22 target pistol.

He snatched the weapons from the cabinet, handed the shotguns to Durso, and was headed back to the women when time ran out.

Through the walls he heard the crash of splintering glass.

It came from the lab. . . .

Chapter 7

Durell chucked the weapons and ran toward the lab.

"What is it, in heaven's name?" Muncie had caught sight of him just before he'd turned. He heard a clatter of heels as she and Tina joined Durso, hurrying after him.

He didn't bother to reply; dread twisted his gut like a cord. The sound of shattering glass continued to come from the lab as he approached. He brought out his revolver, hardly knowing what to expect.

He stopped at the lab door, remembering Maj. Miller's prohibition against opening it, and peered through the little window. Dimly his eyes made out the form of the major struggling with someone at the end of the room. He could do nothing but watch; there was no telling what had been loosed in there. The major was hardly a powerhouse, but neither was his assailant, a small, lightly built man in green clothing. Durell guessed that the intruder had meant to steal Dr. Plettner's notes and had surprised Maj. Miller, but now he was paying for it. The soldier had him down and was bludgeoning him.

When the man in green lay still, the major rose unsteadily. He caught sight of Durell, and called through the door, "Stay out. I've been exposed. Get out of the house. It's got to burn!" He saw the look on Durell's face. "It's just a matter of minutes for me anyhow, Sam," he called.

"What's he doing in there!" It was Muncie, indignant.

"The man's mad. What's he talking about?" Durso demanded.

"Shut up! Get back!" Durell shoved them away and turned back to Maj. Miller, who had sunk to his knees.

"I don't understand—is he. . . ?" Her blue eyes were round with alarm.

"Dying," Durell said. "It's your husband's work." Angrily he pushed through the others.

"Where are you going?" she asked. "You're not really going to . . . to do what he said?"

"Of course not," Durso exclaimed. "It's insane, I tell you. It's Dr. Plettner's laboratory, his data—Caske property!"

Durell offered to reason, but only for a second. "Suppose whatever's in there got loose in a city!"

"It won't, it can't . . . I mean. . . !" Muncie stammered.

"You mean you don't want it to, but that won't stop it. Get out of the way."

Durso stepped haughtily before him. "I won't allow this," he insisted.

Durell hit him, the blow coming out of rage and frustration with volcanic force, and Durso bounced off a wall and landed on his back. He looked up with stunned eyes as Durell stepped over him, bound for the fireplace in the living room. Muncie and Tina followed, then Durso, holding a bruised jaw.

"Please Mr. Durell . . . Sam?" Muncie clasped his arm, holding him back. "At least call a doctor for the man, before you—"

"There isn't a phone, and it wouldn't matter if there were. All you'd get would be a dead doctor."

The handyman and maid were waiting in the living room, eyes wide at all the hubbub. "Phineas and Joanna, come here,'' Durell said. He looked over his shoulder. Durso shambled into the room. "Get over here," he told him.

With everyone gathered around, Durell spoke rapidly. "This is what we're going to do: Take weapons and slip into the jungle. Head for the airstrip where the jet is to land. If it can't take all of us in the morning, it can send another, with help, if need be.''

"That man in the lab—there are others?'' Muncie asked. Her eyes were round, frightened.

"I'm sure of it; we're lucky if we've got two, three minutes before they hit the place. They may have heard the fight, too.'' He took a breath. "We're going to get out of here in two groups to attract less attention. Durso will take his wife, and Phineas will escort Mrs. Plettner and Joanna.'' He began distributing the guns found in the library. "Use these only if you have to.''

"Lordy, I couldn't shoot anybody,'' Joanna said.

"You may change your mind before you reach that airstrip,'' Durell replied. "If you have to shoot, shoot to kill.''

They stared at him dumbly, and he was made to recognize the differences between him and them. He accepted killing as a real alternative; it was an essential tool in his business—nothing more, nothing less. It didn't seem a real possibility to them—to them he was talking make-believe.

They'd find out.

Only Muncie and Durso accepted the situation with a measure of aplomb—they were good at masking their feelings.

Muncie told him, "If I have to go, I want my Weatherby.''

"It's in the major's room. Hurry.''

She rushed away with a rustle of silk.

Durso had recovered enough to argue again. "Suppose there's only one person out there—or none? Is all this artillery necessary? Why don't we just get us some lights and go get him?''

"It could be a dozen, that's why,'' Durell said. Nothing more was said in the seconds it took Muncie to return. Tension showed on everyone's face. Phineas put an arm around Joanna's shoulder. When Muncie returned, Durell asked her the location of the least exposed exit.

"Kitchen," she said. She led the way.

"Stay away from lighted windows," he told them as he stood ready at the door. "Don't silhouette yourself."

"I'm scared, Mr. Durell." It was Joanna.

"We can't stay in this house. It's that simple," he said, his voice stern. Turning to Durso, he said, "You and Tina . . . go now!" Durso sounded cocky. "See you at the airstrip in the morning, Durell—if I don't accidentally blow your head off in the dark."

Durell didn't trouble with a reply. He asked that the kitchen light be turned off, and when that was done, cracked the door. He felt Durso, then Tina, slide into the darkness.

"Phineas?"

"Right here, Mr. Durell."

"Out you go. Joanna? Muncie? Stick with him."

Phineas brushed past him, then the softer form of Joanna, out into the window night.

Then he felt the sharp prod of a rifle muzzle against the back of his neck. . . .

"Don't try anything this time, or you won't have a head left for Ron to blow off," Muncie told him. She spoke in a tone of nervous strain. "You're not going to burn my house down."

"If I don't, lots of people may die. Don't try to stop me," he said.

"Get out that door," she ordered.

"I'm not going. I can't." He turned slowly, careful not to startle her, and felt the muzzle slide from his neck. The room wasn't totally dark; starlight layered shadow on shadow. He couldn't see the gun, but he could make out the vague lines of Muncie's body. He listened to the noises outside for a second, heard nothing to indicate that the others had run into trouble, was thankful for that, at least. He told Muncie, "I'm going to fire this place. You'll have to kill me to stop it."

"No!"

He walked past her, unpleasantly aware that she kept her rifle trained on him.

"Come back!" she demanded.

He ignored her, striding into the living room. She followed him. "I'm warning you," she said. He heard her throw the bolt of her rifle.

The lights remained on in the living room; he got a good look at her and felt a fleeting touch of remorse. She trembled and tears dripped down her cheeks. Her eyes were begging him, but he knew what he had to do. "Now's your best chance to get out of here like the others," he told her. "When the fire starts, everything's going to blow sky-high."

He turned to the fireplace, chose a flaming stick, and went over to the window drapes and set them on fire.

Muncie screamed with rage, and he heard the Weatherby's report. Its roar seemed to shake the walls; its slug whiffed by his ear and out a window.

"You little idiot!" He grabbed the rifle from her shaking hands. Flames clawed hungrily up the drapes and licked across the ceiling. Smoke was filling the room.

"Listen!" she told him, eyes wide.

From outside came shouts, mingling with the noise of the wind. He couldn't tell who it was, but it didn't sound good. Everything would have to be done faster now, with less chance of success. There were two oil-filled hurricane lamps; without further word, he took one and smashed it against the floor. He lit the kerosene with another flaming brand and fire reared up, bolting right and left. All of a sudden the hot smoke was suffocating.

Still holding the rifle, he clutched the other lamp and yelled to Muncie over the sizzle and snap of the spreading flames. "Slip into the woods. Head for the airstrip. I'll see you there."

"What are you going to do?" she shouted.

"I have to make sure the lab is burned." He headed out of the flaming room. Smoke swirled; his eyes and lungs stung. He heard Muncie's cough behind him.

Then a door flew open and a man burst through, toting a

short, Soviet-made PPS submachine gun. Durell recognized the Cuban insignia on his beret. Without time to aim the Weatherby, Durell speared the muzzle into the man's gut. He doubled over, and Durell's knee caught him flush in the face. He heard the crunch of bone. The Cuban looped over onto his back.

"Sam. . . !" Muncie reached for him, as if to pull him back into the living room.

He thrust the rifle into her hands, startling her. She looked quickly at it, then back to him, seemingly wondering how he could trust her with it.

"You can't stop what's happening now," he snapped. "Get the hell out!"

She ran for the kitchen.

The last he saw, she was enveloped in smoke. He hoped she made it.

He got to the lab with the other lamp, took a quick peek through the door window. The major lay on the floor near his assailant, whether conscious or unconscious, dead or alive, he couldn't tell. Durell looked away, collected himself, twisted the wick mechanism out of the lamp's base, and poured kerosene over the door, then in the rooms that adjoined the lab. When the glass was empty, he struck a match and set fire racing through the rooms.

With his pistol in hand, he fled outside through the nearest door, keeping low, darting for the jungle. Someone flitted across his path, apparently without seeing him. It wasn't anyone from the house. Gunfire mixed with the roar of the flames and wind. He didn't know whether they were shooting at him or blindly into the building. He couldn't see where the shots came from.

Everything was in wavering fire colors that glowed against stone and foliage.

A machine gun stuttered; slugs wailed.

He felt sudden fear for Muncie and the others. Maybe they were the targets.

There came a *whoosh!* as something exploded, probably a container of laboratory gas. The jungle wall went bright; he felt heat on the back of his neck, heard a scream. Then he was among the trees, where he dropped onto his knees and fought for breath. For a moment he felt sick at what he'd had to do, sick and weary and disgusted, but he came out of it. What he'd done may have saved the lives of countless others. Maj. Miller had known the stakes when he went into the lab.

He held the .38 loosely, watching through the trees. No one had come into the bushes after him. Fire billowed out windows from one end of the house to the other, from eaves and the roof. The glow of the flames reflected on an enormous column of smoke and blowing cinders.

Three men ran toward the house—more Cubans. One waited on guard as the other two rushed into a smoking doorway. Were they going to try to pull out the contents of the lab? If they did, it would be the end of them. Durell wondered if the Russians were here, or had left the dirty work entirely to the Cubans.

He judged they'd gotten wind of Plettner's disappearance and had drawn the same conclusion as the Americans—namely, that it made him suspect number one for what had happened aboard the *Sun Rover*. And that the newly created agent he'd used, or clues to its nature, could be found in his lab.

With the lab destroyed and Plettner still missing, they'd try to squeeze the secret out of Muncie—if they could.

Now it was urgent not only to find and stop Plettner, but to keep his wife out of Soviet hands.

For starters, he'd have to get her safely off the island.

"Mr. Durell?"

He gave a start, nerves popping like elastic.

It was Phineas.

He looked beyond the handyman, saw none of the others. "What are you doing here?"

The young black man spoke in a West Indian singsong. "I came back for Mrs. Muncie. Don't worry about Joanna; she's a long way off—"

"Durso and Tina; did they get away?"

"I didn't see them after I left the house." Phineas took a frightened breath. "Mr. Durell, these people got Mrs. Muncie!"

"Oh, no," Durell groaned. The way things had gone so far, it figured.

"What can we do?" Phineas said. "We can't go away and leave her."

"You're right. There's only one thing to do," Durell said. He got up, brushing his knees. "Let's get her back."

Chapter 8

"I saw them grab her," Phineas said. "I was coming back for her. They hauled her into the bushes around by the garage."

Durell wondered when anything would go right. "Let's have a look," he said. "Stay close to me and keep low." He began working his way further into the shadows, pushing with outstretched arms through the thick foliage. If he didn't pick up Muncie's trail right away, he would head for the beach, he decided. The Cubans must have landed on the lee side of the island in order to avoid the combers that swept the eastern beaches. He remembered the rocky overlook from which Muncie had taken potshots at him. It offered the best vantage for scanning the shore.

Trees hissed and sent up orange banners of steam as they baked in the heat from the burning dwelling. Durell and Phineas beat their way through the clutching growth, following a curved line that would take them by the corner of the garage, where Durell hoped to pick up Muncie's trail.

The firelight flickered through the basketry of tree limbs, playing tricks on him. Every sense was raw with expectancy, alert to the wrong movement of a shadow, a noise that didn't fit . . . anything. . . .

He had no idea how many Cubans were here, or just where any of them were.

Any moment could bring an encounter.

He had to wonder how long he could evade the bulk of them if they chose to hunt him down on this postage-stamp-size hunk of rock.

Anything less than all night wouldn't do.

He was near the garage now. "Show me where you saw her," he told Phineas.

"About there." The man pointed a lanky arm.

Durell pushed his way to the spot, looked this way and that. "It's useless to try to pick out their trail in this light," he said.

"Look here." Phineas stooped and came up with the scope-mounted Weatherby. "It's her gun, Mr. Durell."

Durell spoke with renewed urgency. "Let's get to the beach. Bring that rifle."

In darkness, even with Phineas's familiarity with the island, it took about twenty minutes to reach the pier where he had landed that morning and another five to find his way onto the jutting stones of the headland. He was below the touch of the tradewind now, and nothing tempered the still, wet heat or blew away the mosquitoes.

He crept with extra care out of the trees and among the pitted boulders, inching his way to the lip of a low bluff overhanging the sea. The water below was oily black, almost indistinguishable from the sky it mimicked.

Phineas's low voice was lilting. "I don't know how we can find her in the dark, except if we step on them and get ourselves killed."

"I'd be happier if she'd reached the airstrip," Durell replied. He swung his gaze in a slow arc, watching with the light-sensitive corners of his eyes. Nothing registered on the first scan.

On the second, he saw it.

To the west, several hundred yards offshore, rode the dark, low silhouette of a submarine. It had the stepped outline-conning tower of a "Whisky" class diesel, he thought. He couldn't be positive; everything was black on black. Even as he watched, a white curl rose around the superstructure, and it submerged.

Anxiety broke out in him.

What if they had Muncie in there and were headed for Cuba?

He told himself not to jump to conclusions. It was just as likely that the sub had dived as a precautionary measure to await the return of its landing party. After all, these were American territorial waters. And the blazing structure could call unwonted attention from the mainland. Besides, it seemed unlikely that Muncie's party could have reached the beach and paddled to the sub in the short time since she'd been captured.

He turned to the void in the night that was Phineas and told him to lead the way to the nearest beach west of there. They had to backtrack around a salt swamp in what seemed total blackness, and his clothing was torn and soaked with slime when they came out onto a narrow crescent of sand leading to what he hoped would prove to be the Cubans' landing area.

If they hadn't left already, they would probably bring Muncie here.

He stopped, listening to the night. Wavelets purled sullenly against the sand. The wind made a sound high above them. Insects creaked and chimed.

He whispered to Phineas, told him to stay put until he returned, then moved on. He kept close to the shadows that marked a wall of dense foliage bordering the beach.

Sweat trickled down his ribs.

His steps marked the sand without a sound.

At about the place he'd estimated, a lone sentry was standing guard over three rubber boats. They had been pulled out of the water and deposited in the tree line, but about half of their length projected back onto the sand. He guessed they were four-man dinghies, which would normally have brought twelve men ashore, but they could have been crowded with more.

He regarded the sentry through narrowed eyes. The man seemed alert, perhaps nervous. He was on his feet, moving here and there as if hearing things, stopping, trying to see, moving again. Perhaps he was expecting the return of the landing party.

A quirk of terrain or air brought the sound of the burning house crackling through the woods.

The night held a brooding presence, an intangible aura of death and evil.

Durell moved well into the foliage. Starlight hung in faint shards among the treetops. He picked each step with deliberate care, like a tightrope walker testing his weight. Two minutes passed, then five. He didn't rush it; he stalked with the patience of a lynx. He recognized a movement in the night ahead as the sentry, visible again from just behind the edge of the jungle.

Durell moved within six feet of him, then a yard. . . .

He had a choice of weapons, for he'd been taught how to kill with anything handy. Not all methods were equally sure; in the darkness a finger could miss, or a vertebra refuse to snap.

He chose simply to crush the man's skull with the butt of his pistol.

He lifted his gun and swung with all his might. He felt bone shatter as the impact of the blow jarred through his wrist, up to his elbow.

The sentry's legs folded; he dropped straight down, without a sound.

Durell got under him and dragged him quickly into the bushes. He took a pair of curved PPS magazines from the webbed belt the man wore and went back and picked up his submachine gun. Next, he hauled the dinghies down the sand, leaving them near the water's edge. He hurried, because he had no idea when to expect the return of the raiding party.

A glance out to sea revealed no sign of the sub; it probably was hovering at periscope depth, awaiting the signal of a flare or blinker.

Durell trotted down the beach, sweeping his fingers through the fringe of the water to rinse sticky blood from them. He kept going along the wall of jungle blackness until he came to Phineas.

"Where you been?" Phineas asked.

"Getting rid of their sentry." He showed Phineas the submachine gun. "Let's get into the trees and wait. Do you see where I put their boats?"

Phineas nodded. "How are we going to get Mrs. Muncie?" he asked.

Durell spoke matter-of-factly. "Our only chance is to kill as many of them as we can, before they know what's hit them. We get them disorganized, maybe scattered, then we'll drive in and grab her. Surprise is the key." He couldn't find Phineas's face in the darkness.

"I don't think I can do that, Mr. Durell. I don't think I have the stomach for it," Phineas told him.

"You have to, Phineas," Durell said.

"No. I—I can't. I'm sorry. Maybe I could kill someone if they were trying to kill me, but just to shoot those men when they come on the beach—it's like murder, Mr. Durell."

Durell held back his anger. The world was crumbling all around them, and he had no one but amateurs to help him stop it. He didn't argue; he just said, "You have to do it."

There wasn't any reply.

Durell continued, "We should be able to pick out Mrs. Plettner fairly easily, even in the dark. The Weatherby has a first-rate scope; starlight's bright enough to use it. I'll pick off whoever is holding her or has her covered. I hope she thinks to run for it when I fire. I'm moving on down the beach. I'll be very close, so I won't miss. When she's out of the way or finds cover, you open up with this." Durell pushed the Soviet-made PPS into the handyman's rough grasp. "The safety's up on the clip housing. Feel it? Here are a couple of extra magazines."

"Mr. Durell, I—"

Durell stopped him with a touch. "I'm going now," he told him. "I'm counting on you."

He went down the beach and found a place some thirty yards from the boats, from which he could fire on them most accurately. The hulk of a wind-thrown palm trunk afforded him good protection. At this range the Cubans would be impossible to miss.

He'd just gotten settled when he heard them approaching close behind. Smatters of Spanish came through the crunching of twigs and slapping of branches. They seemed to be making no effort at concealment. He froze, waiting. Sweat pushed through the pores of his face; he held his breath.

"No me gusta." Something had upset one of the Cubans.

He heard low voices. One of them said not to worry: *"No se preocupe. Todo está bien."*

They must have realized their sentry was missing. The curt imperative of an order came to his ears. They were going to search the area; he wouldn't have a chance if they found him. Surprise was all he had to make up for lack of numbers.

He slipped the safety on his rifle to *off*.

The crunch of clumsy footsteps came nearer, grew louder. . . .

From further away came a cry of alarm, shouts back and forth.

They must have found the dead sentry.

Durell shouldered the rifle, bracing a forearm on the trunk of the fallen palm tree, as the Cubans came running onto the beach in a ragged cluster, like flushed birds. He counted six, the last one pulling Muncie along. It meant others were still abroad on the island, but he'd worry about them later. These were thoroughly alarmed. They seemed intent only on reaching their boats and putting out to sea while they still could.

The scene was aswirl with movement and confusion, but the starry reflection on the ocean silhouetted the Cubans nicely, as Durell had known it would. He pulled the trigger with confidence.

The flat sound of the shot echoed across the water as the first of the Cubans fell.

Durell chambered another cartridge, aimed, squeezed.

A second figure collapsed.

There was pandemonium. Bewildered cries. A submachine gun began chattering blindly at the jungle.

Durell was yelling, working the bolt, sweat in his eyes. "Muncie! Run, Muncie!"

His name came back from her as a terrified plea: *"Sam?"*

"Run!" he shouted. He fired again, saw her break away and run into the woods.

What had happened to Phineas? He should have begun raking the Cubans with the submachine gun the instant Muncie had put a few steps between them and herself. Durell knew he couldn't hold them back alone for long.

The Cubans, now prone on the sand, were beginning to get the range. The palm trunk shivered under the thud of their bullets, and the air buzzed and hummed, as if he'd stuck his head into a beehive.

He was beginning to think he'd be lucky to crawl away without catching a slug. He squirmed into the jungle, almost sightless amid the rot and dank rootings of vines and trees. He'd gone perhaps ten feet when the firing stopped. He heard a shouted command and knew they were coming after him.

Jumping to his feet, he began beating his way frantically through the vegetation. Noise didn't matter so much now— distance was the thing. Besides, he counted on them making so much noise they weren't likely to hear him.

Complicating matters was Muncie. He heard her call his name. She was somewhere nearby. He had to get her to safety or all his efforts would have been wasted. He angled toward the source of the sound. She must have heard him coming, because she was headed for him when they ran into each other. She didn't recognize him immediately and started to scream, but he clapped a hand over her mouth and quieted her.

Her ribs shuddered against him, from the beating of her heart. She watched him through the dusky light, eyes wide as he removed his hand. Her voice was hoarse and trembling. "Thank heavens you came!" she said.

"Where can we hide?" he asked.

"I know a place. Hurry." She tugged him by the hand.

He heard the Cubans through the brush no more than fifty feet away and cursed Phineas as he fled behind Muncie. She knew the island thoroughly and soon brought him to a trail where they quickened their pace, but the Cubans hung on tenaciously. They were using flashlights. He could have picked one off, but it wasn't worth revealing himself.

Muncie knew the way, but she couldn't move fast enough.

Yet they had to break contact with the Cubans, or, outnumbered and outgunned, they were sure to die.

Muncie's panting was a high, brushing sound that rode above his own harsh breathing.

She led him up an overgrown stone staircase, and above, he saw the gleaming of what he'd seen from the boat on his arrival: a tumbledown plantation house atop a low hill.

Running up the steps ahead of him, she spoke over her shoulder. "Secret passage inside—they'll never—"

A stunning brilliance cut her words off.

The blinding glare of the submarine's spotlight had lanced through the night to expose them mercilessly on the wide white steps.

From the darkness beyond the dazzle Durell heard in Spanish: "There they are!"

And then, in dismay, the order to fire. . . .

Chapter 9

Durell and Muncie stood out like flies in the harsh glare of the spotlight. Caught in a blazing fraction of time, motion frozen, no place to hide, they made perfect targets, and Durell had a fleeting second to foretaste death.

A machine gun thundered; he flinched, heard a scream.

There was a clattering of metal against stone. . . .

He was still alive!

He could almost touch the stunned silence of the moment. The halo of light that had held him slipped questioningly downward, revealing four dead Cubans—and Phineas, who stood over them with his smoking weapon.

"Phineas!" Muncie called joyously.

His face jerked toward her, gleaming blackly in the brilliance, and in the same instant, faster than the eye could follow, an immense arc of fiery tracer shells squirted from the resurfaced submarine and showered the area where Phineas stood. Twenty-three mm. bullets ripped the handyman to shreds. The torrent of steel kicked and tossed his bloody remains about in a swirl of dust and shrapnel.

It gave Durell the moment he needed, and he hurled himself up the remaining steps into the tumbledown plantation manor, dragging Muncie after him. He'd expected her to be nearly hysterical, but she must have had deep reserves of nerve—or maybe she was just numb after all she'd been through. Stars shone their pale radiance through gaps in the roof as Sam and Muncie stepped cautiously through the trash of the abandoned building. The sound of their movements echoed in the empty rooms.

"Phineas . . ." she said.

"He did what had to be done," Durell told her.

"I don't understand what's happening." She sounded lost and forlorn.

He didn't waste any time with it. "I've tried to explain it," he said shortly. "Where's this secret passage you told me about?" He glanced over his shoulder. "There are still Cubans on the island. The sub may send more, too," he told her.

She led him over a sagging floor that squeaked and trembled; he made out the bare lines of what must have once been a grand staircase. Behind it she opened a door that moaned on rusty hinges. They descended wooden steps in total darkness.

The musty odor of a cellar closed around his nostrils.

He could hear the rustle of her silken garments.

There came the click of a cigarette lighter, and he saw in the glow of its flare that she was taking a candle from a shelf. She lit the candle and held it up to him, looking over the flame with an enigmatic gaze. Her cheeks were smudged, her expensive clothing torn, ruined.

"Sam—may I call you that?"

"Mrs. Plettner . . ." he began.

"Muncie. Hold me? Please?" She leaned against him. He felt her trembling sigh. "Thanks. Thanks for saving me," she said into his shoulder.

"It was in my own interest," he said.

"I suppose so. I don't seem to care why very much. I'm

still alive, thank God. That's all that matters to me.'' She lifted her face up to him. ''Is that wrong?'' she asked.

''No. I hope you'll help me find your husband,'' he said. ''We haven't much time.''

''Honestly, he's not . . . whatever you seem to think he is—he's not bad.''

He regarded her closely and said nothing. She looked away. He said, ''I hope that's true.''

She turned and began leading him down a servants' staircase, speaking as she went. ''He can't help his drinking,'' she said. ''His life—our life together—has been ruined by the Caske company, by all the pressures. . . .''

They entered a spacious kitchen replete with a huge wood-burning iron range. Cobwebs massed among termite-riddled beams. Dust and mildew covered everything. Next came a big pantry with floor-to-ceiling cabinets. Muncie pressed a hidden spring and a cabinet pivoted, revealing a secret doorway. A cool draft flooded out of the opening, wagging the candle flame. Durell followed Muncie inside and pulled the door closed behind them. Again they descended, this time on steps cut from the living stone. Drops of water plinked and plunked.

Muncie said, ''They say that the man who built this used the money he'd stolen as a pirate—this was back in the sixteen hundreds—and that he made his prisoners dig this tunnel, then killed them.''

''Who else knows about it?'' Durell asked.

''I don't know. Not many. See over there? Skeletons.'' She pointed with the candle.

They passed a row of bones scattered at the foot of the wall. Damp calcium deposits left by dripping water hung like icicles from vacant eye sockets and gaping jaws.

''Let's hope we don't join them,'' he said. ''Where does the tunnel go?''

''To the sea. It comes out in a water grotto. You've got to swim the last ten yards or so.''

''Near the landing beach?''

''Pretty close. I guess that isn't good, is it?''

Durell paused. ''Let's find a spot to sit. The sub is certain

74

to leave by dawn. The Russians wouldn't want to get caught in these waters.''

"The tunnel widens into a room—I call it the treasure room," she said. "It isn't far."

They soon came to the widened section of the tunnel, where they sat down to rest in soft dust that had accumulated for centuries. Muncie stood the candle in the dust and leaned back against the wall, next to Durell. "I'm exhausted," she said. Her voice saddened. "Poor Phineas . . ." She shook her head as if to shake the memory of his death from her mind. "Let's talk about something else. Can't you tell me more? What's happened to bring you here? And then those others?"

Durell held her gaze. "All I can tell you is it's bad," he said. "Worse than you can imagine. A nightmare."

"What was in the lab? What killed Maj. Miller?"

"Don't you know? Can't you guess?"

She shook her head. "Honestly . . ." she said. "He shouldn't have broken in there in any case."

"I helped him." He took her hands. "And I hope you'll help me, Muncie. I'm going to Geneva with Durso tomorrow—"

"Why?"

"Geneva was like a second home to your husband, wasn't it? To you, too. It's the next logical place to try and pick up his trail."

She spoke a little too quickly. "You won't find anything."

He considered her pale face by the light of the candle. She didn't flinch, but she looked wary. He saw that she needed gentleness, patience. But he hadn't time for either. "I'm going," he told her. "If you come and help, I'll find your husband faster and save lives. If you don't, I'll still find him, but there'll be more Maj. Millers."

"I don't know what to do," she said uncertainly.

"It seems clear to me," he said.

"I may ruin his career with Caske."

"A lot more than his career is at stake," Durell replied. "Another thing: The Russians are after you. They were behind the attack tonight."

"Why?"

"They don't know that Dr. Plettner locked you out of his laboratory. They probably think you know almost as much about what went on in it as he does."

Understanding dawned in her blue eyes. "Then that's why they tried to kidnap me."

"They're sure to come after you again, even if we get away from here," he told her. "Maybe not with guns—maybe through a friend. They're devious. They'll stop at nothing."

She shivered, looking apprehensively over her shoulder, and moved against him. He felt her warmth, the soft curve of her hip.

He said, "I can't leave you here, that's for sure. If you won't come to Geneva, I'll have to take you to Washington under protective custody."

"That doesn't sound bad, after your description of the Russians," she replied.

"But I need you with me in Geneva," he insisted.

She gave him a tight, grim smile. "At least someone needs me," she said, with sadness and a touch of resignation. "It wasn't only Peter's infidelity, not just my anger with Tina and Ron that made me bitter, Sam. I couldn't seem to feel anything good anymore—I guess I was cut off by hatred. I—I didn't love Peter anymore." She seemed to be looking for understanding in his eyes. "Not really," she said.

He watched her and said nothing.

She snuggled closer and laid her head against his shoulder, as if the admission had relaxed her. She felt good against him, and he put an arm around her shoulders. "It feels good—so good—not to be lonely for a while," she said with a sigh, "even if I'm only with a stranger in this—this hole in the ground." A touch of bitterness returned in her little laugh.

Nothing happened for a few seconds, as he held her gently and watched the wax drip from their candle. The smell of the wax came in warm currents through the cool air.

Then, without further preliminaries, she gave him a kiss on the cheek.

It was a pleasant surprise, but distracting. He turned to tell her so, but she closed her eyes and puckered her lips, and he thought, What the hell?

She responded with something like wanton hunger as he pressed his lips against hers.

He was aware of the heat of her breasts, the yearning in her embrace.

There was no mistaking that she wanted to be loved by him.

He was afraid it was for the wrong reasons—that she was using the moment in rebellion, as a way of lashing out at the husband who had failed her—breaking the bonds to an unhappy past. Even her kiss showed anger; he felt the sharp edge of her teeth and the stab of long fingernails into the muscles of his back.

She smelled of perfume and sachet. Over her hot breathing he heard the hollow whisper of wind and wave, brought from the sea by the tunnel that stretched away.

Durell was of two minds: tempted by the sheer erotic magnetism of Muncie, but concerned lest the flood of her inner furies drown them both.

He was on the point of saying something sensible when, whispering an invitation into his ear, she moved his hand to cover her trembling breast.

After that, rational thought wouldn't have been easy.

But before he could relax, something new brought them both upright.

"Miss Muncie!"

It was the voice of Joanna, the maid. *"They say you'd better give up, or they're going to come in after you!"*

Muncie gave a horrified gasp. "They've caught Joanna!" She stared at Durell.

"We can't do much about it," he said.

The maid's voice echoed down the tunnel. *"Please come out! They're hurting me!"*

Muncie stirred; Durell held her back. "I can't let them harm her," she told him.

"You haven't any choice," he said. He listened. "If she

knows how to get in here, I suppose she knows where the tunnel comes out. . . ."

"I don't know . . . maybe. . . ." Muncie looked frightened.

"Then the Cubans may have that covered, too." Durell chewed his lip. Worry settled like ice in his gut. "Is there another way?" he asked.

Muncie shook her pale face. "Maybe if I just went and explained to them that I don't know anything. . . ."

Durell shook his head gravely. "It won't work; they've got themselves in too deep to believe it. Look at it from their side—it might have looked easy when they started, but everything's turned sour. The lab's burned with every secret in it; they've had casualties, time's running out—and they've got to get out of U.S. waters by morning. And all they can hope for is to take back the famous doctor's assistant. It's turned into a nightmare. After all that, you think you're going to convince them that they made a mistake, turn away, and walk off?" He took a breath. "If they get their hands on you, they'll torture you to death before they'll accept your story," he said.

Joanna screamed, a long hair-raising shriek that ended in a gasping gurgle.

"Dear God!" Muncie whimpered.

He saw he had to get her away from it; she'd go to pieces. He took her hand and rose from the dust. "Come on, let's go to the grotto and have a look," he suggested, taking the candle.

It was some fifty twisting yards to where the tunnel came out on a wet shelf of stone that barely lay above the level of the water. When high tide flooded in, it would cover the shelf and the walls up to Durell's neck, to judge by water stains around the room. The entrance was little more than a crack, barely wide enough for him to squeeze through. Even as he inspected it, his nose was stung by the first whiff of tear gas. . . .

He pulled Muncie roughly toward the exit. "Hurry, let's get out of here," he barked.

"What . . . what if someone's out there . . . waiting?"

His voice was edged with impatience. "We can take our chances. Or sit here and choke on tear gas. Or maybe drown when the tide comes in. I'd rather take our chances out there." He cast his jacket aside.

"Listen," she said.

He stopped and cocked his ear to the outside. For the first time he noticed a hollow booming, muffled through the stone and water, but distinct.

"What do you think it is?" she asked.

"There's only one thing I can think of," he said, his spirits plummeting. "Waves against steel—water against a boat's hull . . ."

Muncie touched the base of her throat, eyes wide. "The submarine . . ." she gasped.

Her hand trembled in Durell's. "What are we going to do?" she asked. She coughed. The tear gas was thickening.

"Go out under water. It's our only option." His eyes stung. He slipped off the ledge into the warm water. His feet didn't touch bottom. He could see nothing beneath the sheen of reflection on the surface, laid by the candle. He held out his hand, and she sat on the ledge, then slid in beside him.

Her face showed fear, but she sounded resolute enough. "Watch out for the currents," she told him.

"What about them?"

"There are underwater pockets and caverns along the shore. If the currents carry you into one, you'll never find your way out—you'll drown for sure." Her eyes were becoming bloodshot from the tear gas.

"When you get outside, go to the left," he told her. "Find the shore. Get in among the rocks. If I'm not there, wait. If I don't show up in a little while, head for the airstrip yourself."

"What are you going to do?"

"Nothing, but we may get separated in the darkness. One of us could have bad luck. That sub's out there to stop us, you know."

"I'm scared," she said.

"So am I. Let's go." He gulped a lungful of air, ducked

under, and grasping the sides of the crevice, pulled himself through.

The water outside was only a shade lighter than the ocean bottom, and Durell swam through a vague twilight provided by the radiance of the stars. He was a powerful swimmer under normal conditions, but the poison in his lungs felt as if it were eating him alive. He went to the left, as he'd told Muncie to do, but realized now that he had no idea in which direction the sub lay.

The ringing of waves against its steel plate still sounded in his ears. Then he became aware of another noise, an intermittent grinding that reverberated through the water.

Slowly and carefully, he broke the surface, blew the fire from his lungs, and gulped the sweetness of fresh air.

The Russian submarine was some two hundred yards away. Its searchlight was on, but unaccountably blazed into the sky from atop a conning tower that leaned at a crazy angle.

For a moment he could not understand what had happened. Then the grinding thunder he'd heard made sense—the submarine must have run aground.

Fascinated, he watched for something to tell him what was happening, how such a thing could have transpired. The shaft of the searchlight didn't waver. There was no movement at all—no sound except for the awful ringing of waves and grinding of stone.

Then the whole horror of what must have happened fell on him with crushing terror.

He swam quickly to shore and shouted into the darkness for Muncie, no longer bothering with concealment.

"Sam! Over here!" Her voice came back out of the trees.

He crawled from the water, slipping over stones and boulders. A faint glow from beyond the hill showed that the Plettner compound was still burning. There was a heavy odor of smoke.

He slogged up to solid ground and sat down, coughing the tear gas from his lungs. Muncie's feet crunched through gravel. "Here I am," she said.

The sub's spotlight sizzled into the sky.

"We're still alive," she said. "I can't believe it."

"It's our lucky night," he said.

"I don't understand why the submarine didn't try to stop us. Why wasn't the spotlight turned on the grotto? What's going on?" she asked.

"The crew's dead," Durell told her in a matter-of-fact voice. He felt a shiver. "Come on, let's get away from here." He took her hand and pulled her into the woods.

"But how. . . ?"

"The bug. From the lab."

"You mean it's spread over the island already?" she said in alarm.

"No. Maj. Miller said it couldn't spread far through the air; it'll die quickly if it isn't in a culture—or a body." He pressed on through the woods. Muncie followed as best she could, still hanging onto his hand. "The bacteria must have been carried aboard the sub," he said.

"But how?"

"I saw a couple of them run into the house, probably hoping to salvage some of your husband's material. They weren't with the group that took you. They must have gotten infected, then contaminated the sub, killing its crew." They were rounding the hill on the side away from the plantation house. Now that they'd escaped out the back door of the tunnel, the Cuban commandos weren't likely to catch up with them. They'd have to return to the sub before dawn, and they'd die there. The unfortunate Joanna was already dead, to judge by what he'd heard in the tunnel.

He told Muncie to take the lead and show him where the airplane was expected to land in the morning.

"What will they do with the submarine—the victims?" she asked.

"It'll have to be towed away and sunk. We'll have to quarantine the island," he said.

She sounded bewildered. "Why would Peter have created such a terrible thing?" she asked.

"Lots of people would like to know the answer to that," Durell replied.

"I just can't believe he did it with any evil intent," she said. She tripped, and he kept her from falling.

The dim light filtering through the trees made her only a shadow in his hands.

"Maybe you're right," he told her. "Maybe we can find out in Geneva—I've got to see Caske again. There's a vaccine, if we can get it. Come with me? Help me?" he asked.

There was a second's pause, then in solemn tones, she replied, "After what's happened here tonight, how could I refuse?"

It was a victory.

Chapter 10

Not twenty-four hours after the events on Plettner's island, Durell's life again hung in the balance.

A killer struck as he and Muncie came out of Geneva's elegant old Hotel Richmond and walked toward their rented Fiat, parked on the Quai du Mont-Blanc, where Lake Léman begins its forty-five-mile reach north between the mountains.

It was early evening, and a thin, chill mist glistened on mansard roofs, iron balconies, and corner cafes reminiscent of Paris.

Durell had had little luck finding the spoor of Dr. Peter Plettner, and the weather hadn't helped his spirits.

He was tired and discouraged, his thoughts turned inward more than usual. Having failed to make any headway independently, he was looking forward to accompanying Muncie to an appointment she had made with Bernhard Caske—he was relying on this ruse to get in to Caske, because he knew the man wouldn't voluntarily give him another hearing.

He'd decided first to plead for the release of information the

83

home office probably held regarding Plettner's genetic engineering projects; it might help American scientists to develop a vaccine. He still hoped Caske would say something that might shed light on the scientist's whereabouts, despite his refusal to help in Washington.

Remembering those who had died, Durell felt he had to get his hands on Plettner soon, one way or the other.

The clock was still running, and nobody knew when it would run out.

Beside him, Muncie was clothed in a new tweed suit and long, down-stuffed stormcoat—she'd replenished her wardrobe with funds from an ample Swiss bank account. She looked none the worse for the terrors of the night before, but a touch of cynical reserve had set about her dusky eyes, as if she'd already begun to harbor second thoughts about this collaboration with him.

He thought briefly about the passion that had blazed between them the night before, then, with some effort, put it out of his mind.

Money had been no problem for him, either. A phone call had brought a shy-looking watchmaker named Nuri Borodin with five thousand dollars out of K Section's Green Fund, on deposit at the Suisse Banque Cantonale de Genève.

Nuri was K Section's Geneva Control.

It was the dinner hour; the raw weather was unpleasant, and the lake and mountains were shrouded in mist. Durell and Muncie were the only pedestrians to be seen.

He heard the wet slap of footsteps catching up from behind and moved aside to let the stranger hurry past.

Muncie screamed.

Durell half turned, snapping his head around to see what had alarmed her—but he saw it too late: the snarling face, the upraised arm. An arc of shining steel gleamed like liquid, and the knife struck against his ribs with full force, just below his upraised arm.

He was aware of the hit, and his heart jumped.

He caught the assailant's forearm, pushed it away, felt nothing as the knife drew back. The edge of Durell's right hand hacked into the bridge of the man's nose, blinding him, and a hard, wrenching twist broke his arm and sent the knife flying. The man stumbled clumsily into Durell, gave a short scream, and collapsed.

Everything had happened in a few seconds.

Shocked, Durell felt under his coat, expecting to draw out a bloody hand. Instead his fingers found a cut in the leather of his shoulder holster. He withdrew his snub-nosed revolver. A gouge on the chamber showed where the knife point had struck.

His heart labored, pulsing with adrenaline; he looked at Muncie.

She stood back staring, dumbfounded.

"More luck," he told her, taking a deep breath.

"Keep your luck for yourself. I want out," she snapped.

"Not until you get me in to see Caske." His tone brooked no argument. He glanced quickly around, bending down to the man he had felled. The walkway was shrouded from view by Brunswick Garden. No one was in sight; no one had seen what had happened.

He felt for the man's pulse. "He's dead," he told Muncie.

"Let's get out of here," she said. "What if someone calls the police?"

"Just a minute." Durell had never seen the man. By the low radiance of foggy streetlamps he went through his pockets, found a wallet with a meaningless name on the papers it contained: Jacques de Gendre, purportedly of French citizenship, a resident of Marseille. He was probably a hired assassin.

Durell replaced the wallet, found a little Beretta in the pocket of the overcoat. He wiped that off and replaced it.

A look at the swollen, misshapen nose gave Durell a hunch about what had caused death: Splinters of the broken nose had been pressed into the man's brain when he'd stumbled against him. Durell would have preferred having him alive to question.

Then he made a discovery that caused some questions to be unnecessary. In another pocket was a photo of himself.

From the background, it obviously had been taken the day before . . . at Dr. Plettner's house.

"It must have been Ron and Tina," Muncie told him.

He urged her away from the corpse. Sparkling mist haloed the streetlamps. "Let's go to the car," he said.

"You should go to Ron and—"

"How do I find him? We haven't seen the Dursos since we landed."

She sounded distraught. "Well, what are you going to do?"

He opened a door for her. "We still have an appointment with Herr Caske. Ron Durso can wait until that's over." He got behind the wheel.

They followed the lakefront past stately nineteenth-century buildings fronting the harbor. The umbrella-shaped trees were bare of leaves. The mist was changing to snow.

He kept an eye on the rearview mirror; the line of headlights behind held nothing out of the ordinary.

"Are you nervous?" Muncie asked. "I am."

He ignored her question, glancing at the luminous dial on his watch. "We should get there in about five minutes," he said.

"I shouldn't have let you talk me into this," she said. She straightened her hem over a pretty knee. "I don't think Mr. Caske is going to be overjoyed. Especially since you asked him for help before and he told you no."

They rode in silence. Durell was considering what to do if Caske refused to help him this time. He felt he couldn't let it go at that. He had the Q Clearance, which meant he could take any measures he deemed necessary. Of course, if he got caught breaking the law, he'd have to pay for it—K Section would disown him.

On the other hand, if he failed to stop Plettner, or whoever had killed the people on the *Sun Rover* . . .

He tried not to think of the consequences.

City lights had fallen behind.

The snow was a white dust slanting across the headlight beams.

Durso or Caske—or both—could be allied with the mysterious Plettner, he decided. Durso's willingness to cooperate could merely have been a cover for his scheming. Indeed, it must have been: Who else could have taken the picture and hired the assassin?

The only other possibility didn't necessarily involve Dr. Plettner, if Caske were that scared of losing industrial secrets that might cost him a great deal to replace.

Would Caske murder to keep his star scientist's work a company secret?

Muncie's voice brought Durell back. She sat primly, looking straight ahead, and she spoke with obvious difficulty. "I'm . . . I'm embarrassed about last night," she said.

He made no reply.

"Maybe we got too close too fast. I feel . . . I *know* I should love Peter. . . ."

"It isn't for me to judge," he said. "Do you?"

"I'm going to try." She turned to him. "People do things they shouldn't when their ship is sinking, or, you know, it's the end of the world."

"Do they?" His world seemed to be ending so often he'd forgotten it was out of the ordinary.

"Be serious," she said. Her eyes pleaded for his understanding.

"I admire your honesty," he told her.

Caske's headquarters were housed in a seventeenth-century stone chalet nestled amid formal gardens against a mountain backdrop. It loomed over the shore of the lake.

A pair of Caske minions met them at the door. They were strapping mountaineer types in business suits. One wore his hair in a crewcut and was named Zinger; his companion, a man with a soldier's stolid, empty face, was Dumid. Durell never heard their first names. They escorted him and Muncie through the antique-furnished halls of the mansion. Despite the hour employees came and went amid Bruges tapestries and paintings by Tintoretto, Titian, and Rubens.

Bald-headed Caske sat at an enormous desk beside a fireplace of baronial proportions. Its mantel was carved with coats of arms.

The sense of power here was tangible, much more so than in Caske's relatively modest Washington office. Durell could only dimly imagine the extent of the shock waves should Caske's financial empire collapse.

But the fear of such a catastrophe was on the man's bearded face, as Caske's hard eyes lit in recognition of Durell. He looked fevered, fretful . . . there was something of the wounded bull in him . . . something of the cornered beast.

Muncie started to speak, but he brushed her aside, addressing Durell. "I didn't expect you here, sir. Muncie, my dear, what's the meaning of this?"

"I brought him as a friend, Mr. Caske. He wants to help me find Peter," she told him.

"You little fool! Get out! Get out, both of you!" He was trembling with rage.

"Disappointed that I'm still alive?" Durell said. "I'm not going anywhere—not until we've talked."

"How dare you?" Caske took a menacing step toward him. "I have spoken with Mr. Ronald Durso today—"

"I'll bet you have—"

"And he informed me of your lawless insistence on appropriating our property—and exactly what was involved in the wanton destruction of Dr. Plettner's laboratory. You'll pay for that!"

Durell kept his voice calm. "My government stands ready to make good your loss—dishes get broken in an emergency. That's what this is, but I don't seem able to make you understand."

"An emergency? You talk as if I have the key to save the world." His whiskered jaw jutted belligerently.

"Maybe you do."

Caske paused, as if to assimilate this. "Then buy it from me—if the emergency is so great."

Durell regarded the cunning eyes with a concealed distaste. "It doesn't hurt to talk," he said. "Send your men out."

"They're mindless robots. I assure you, they'll repeat nothing."

"Maybe that comforts you, Mr. Caske, but I don't believe such a creature walks on two legs. If we're going to talk seriously, it'll have to be in confidence."

Caske hesitated a moment longer. "What about Mrs. Plettner?"

"She goes out, too." Durell said.

"Very well. Zinger, Dumid!" Caske snapped his fingers and pointed toward the door. They exited silently. Muncie went after them, giving Durell an uncertain look

Durell hadn't anticipated playing on Caske's greed. Things had a way of unfolding to one's advantage, provided one was quick enough to see it.

"How much?" Caske asked. He remained standing, his tone combative. "You must realize that I've invested a great deal of money in Dr. Plettner, and I have a right to expect a profit from his efforts."

"You have a right to a profit," Durell said. He glanced about the room. French doors led into a garden. "How much are you asking? Not that we'll necessarily bail you out of bankruptcy."

"Bankruptcy! I forbid the use of that word regarding my affairs, sir! No enterprise of mine will ever go bankrupt. Do you understand?" His big frame bent angrily toward Durell. There was a pause. "Seven hundred million dollars!"

Even though Durell was merely playing a game, the amount jolted him. The government may as well pay the ransom.

"I know the United States wants the material," Caske ranted. "Mr. Durso told me what the variant *coli* did to your thieving colleague and the crew of the submarine." His voice turned cunning and his eyes as cold as the north wall of an alpine peak. "Your government knows it has in the variant *coli* the potential for a superior biological weapon. It also should know that modern weapons are extremely expensive, especially in their development."

Something in Caske's tone made Durell aware of a horrible new threat. "And if we don't buy. . . ?" he questioned.

"Isn't it conceivable that others will?" Caske replied coyly.

That made up Durell's mind: Caske couldn't be reasoned with. What's more, he'd gone from simply refusing to help to, in a sense, doubling the threat the U.S. already faced.

He had to be dealt with immediately.

Plettner's files had to be taken from him—and Durell had already decided on a way to accomplish that.

"Get your coat," he ordered. "You're coming with me."

Caske looked puzzled. "To meet your superiors? Bring them here."

Durell drew his revolver, nerves taut with the knowledge that a lot of help for Caske was just beyond the door. Getting him away might not be easy. "You're a clear danger to humanity," he snarled. "I'd consider killing you for pleasure. So just do as I say and don't ask questions."

Caske's mouth worked with soundless anger as he withdrew his coat from a closet.

Everything seemed to be under control—until Caske threw himself on the floor and yelled, "Help! Help me!"

Chapter 11

Durell wasn't worried about Bernhard Caske. Zinger and Dumid were the problem—they'd come storming through the door any second. Ignoring the sprawled industrialist, he lunged to head them off.

The crewcut Zinger was first, slamming the door back into the wall as he burst in, pawing for his gun.

Beating him by a second, Durell crashed the butt of his revolver into the angle at the man's thick neck and shoulder. Zinger fell headlong, smashing down like a shot buffalo, and Dumid charged in behind him, flailing for Durell with both hands. In a move that was cool and quick Durell caught an arm and cartwheeled him into a wall of books.

Dumid hit the floor, leather-bound volumes cascading around him. He scrambled up, but Durell kicked him in the side of the head, and he sank back and lay still.

"What are you doing!"

His eyes found Muncie rushing in, shocked and angry.

Caske still lay on the floor, hands clasped over his bald head. "He's a madman!" he roared.

"On your feet." Durell toed him. "Hurry."

The man did as he was told, glancing unhappily at his fallen bodyguards. Muncie closed the door abruptly, suddenly aware of how this would look to anyone passing by.

"You haven't a chance of getting away with this," Caske declared.

"So far, so good," Durell replied.

Muncie's face was grim. "You've done it now," she said. "Get your coat."

"Don't help him, I'm warning you," Caske threatened.

"Out the french doors," Durell told him. To Muncie: "You know the way to the car?"

"I think I can find it." She seemed in a daze.

He pushed Caske ahead. "Move!"

Caske went out. "You'll spend the rest of your days in jail," he snarled.

On the patio the air was cold; snow fell through light that shone from the windows of the building. Beyond floated a liquid darkness. Muncie led, then Caske; Durell brought up the rear, his gun aimed at the man's back. A wet glow shone from the skin of Caske's bald head.

The air smelled clean. Cars made a rushing sound along the invisible highway.

Durell glanced back, and saw nothing to indicate that an alarm had been sounded. He hoped to depart peacefully; his quarrel was with Caske, not his employees.

He didn't care to think what might happen to him if he failed now. Life in jail—even a Swiss jail—wasn't pleasant to contemplate.

"Muncie?" he called, seeing the snow-streaked lighting of the parking lot. "Go bring the car here. The less we promenade Mr. Caske, the better."

"My people will find you," Caske said, glowering.

"Why not the police? Or can't your operations stand the scrutiny?" Durell watched Muncie go, his gun held casually.

"I have no fear of the police. Nor do I need them, Herr Durell. You'll see."

Durell glanced over his shoulder: still no pursuit. He couldn't expect Zinger and Dumid to stay out cold all night. Where was Muncie? He peered past Caske, whose black overcoat was becoming encrusted with snow. What if she'd turned on him? What if *she* had been the one who took those photos on the island? If so, the question was *why*. He had no answer—but there wasn't always time for neat answers.

Durell's face was impassive, but his nerves vibrated like shrouds in a rising gale. His concern went beyond his own safety. Caske had as much as said he'd sell Plettner's work to the highest bidder, which made him no better than the monster responsible for the *Sun Rover*.

Waiting, he rubbed the stubble that had sprouted on his chin since he had arrived in Switzerland.

He read the luminous markings on the dial of his watch.

He'd give her another sixty seconds. He'd steal a car if he had to. He dared not wait any longer.

She could've gone to the police, maybe alerted the security guard.

The alarm might be spreading at this very moment. . . .

"Sam?"

She was nearby. He made no reply. Caske watched him quizzically, then rolled his eyes in the direction from which she had spoken. Durell kept his gun on Caske and peered carefully around the corner of the building.

"Sam? Where are you?"

She was closer now. He recognized the movement of a dim figure, snow slanting across his vision. She seemed to be alone.

"Over here," he called in a low voice.

"I thought I'd lost you in this snow." She came up puffing, her cheeks wet and frosty. "I got the car."

"You go first." He trusted no one completely.

She hesitated a fraction, reading his thoughts, he guessed. "Sure," she said.

They went down a slope of lawn. White puffs swirled from

93

their mouths. The car was running, lights off, windshield wipers slapping and sliding. There was no other sound in the large parking lot. A strong breeze came across, stinging Durell's ears. "Get in," he told Caske, indicating the front passenger door.

"I—"

"Shut up, unless you want to chew a handkerchief," Durell snapped. Sullenly, Caske slid into the car. Durell turned to Muncie. He didn't want to leave her; she might still be helpful. But she'd said she wanted out, and now was as good a time as any. "You can stay," he told her.

"I'm in a bit deep to quit now, aren't I?"

"You could say I forced you."

"You think the police would swallow that?"

"It's for you to decide."

"Some decision." She sounded frustrated, but strangely cheerful. "You're stuck with me. I didn't know you were going to kidnap the man. Frankly, it was great to see Caske lying on the floor scared out of his gourd—I'd go to the scaffold for that."

"Don't blame me later," he said. "You sit in the back."

He got behind the wheel, one eye on Caske, and drove north on Route One, which followed the shore of Lake Léman toward Versoix. Caske sat in tight-lipped indignation. The headlamp beams swarmed with zipping snowflakes; the passage of oncoming cars sent snowdust swirling in clouds.

When he had driven some miles, Durell parked at a roadside phone booth and dialed the number of Nuri Borodin at his little fifteenth-century antique shop near the Grand Rue in old Geneva.

"My God, what have you done!" Nuri lamented when Durell told him he'd kidnaped Caske.

"He had to be neutralized. I need someplace to stash him for awhile," Durell said.

"Are you sure about this, Cajun?"

"My responsibility," Durell replied.

Nuri said, "We do have access to a monastery, and it's not far from where you are."

"Where is it?"

"Just beyond Versoix, on the river." Nuri gave him directions.

Durell said: "Can you meet me? I need you to arrange a watch on Caske."

"As you wish." Nuri was as cool as the Alpine night.

"I'm on my way then."

"It's on your head, Cajun."

Durell hung up thinking that Nuri's record was outstanding, but he was no longer bold. Retirement was on his mind. Durell made a mental note to have him rotated to the States; he could spend the last three years of his career in well-deserved safety and comfort—and not get in the way of those who had to take risks to do their jobs.

After all, Nuri was a rare specimen—most K Section agents quit before their thirty-fifth birthday, or were killed. . . .

Durell returned to the car, ignoring Caske's menacing looks, and drove into the snow-muffled village of Versoix. Finding the river road, he followed it through a tilted valley, heading away from the lake. The heater whirred. There was no traffic. They were a moving island in an insubstantial world of darkness. The scent of Muncie's perfume was more real than the nothingness beyond the headlights. She wore a light, fresh scent that reminded him of meadow flowers.

He wondered about the wisdom of bringing her. It was no longer easy to justify on the basis that she might lead him to her husband—they'd already been to every one of Plettner's haunts. Still, there was the long-shot hope that something would jar a memory.

Her bittersweet beauty, the taste of her lips might have been reason enough for most men to keep her with them.

Durell considered women—when he thought of them at all—as dangerous distractions.

A rough wooden sign between stone columns told him he'd arrived at the monastery of the Order of St. Michael. There was a winding drive, potholed and crowded with untrimmed shrubbery, that led through a park studded with trees. It ended at a forbidding stone wall. A wooden gate bound with iron marked the entrance to the monastery. Durell pulled a bell cord, and a door opened in the gate.

"You are M'sieur Durell?" a hooded monk asked.

"*Oui.*"

"I'll show you where to take your guest." The shadow under the hood was darker than the night; the voice dry and rasping. There was a rattling of keys and the big gate opened. Durell heard the monk call to bring the car through.

They parked on cobblestones. Caske got out stiffly, eyes darting. Muncie, seeming fearful, took Durell's arm, pulling closer as they followed behind Caske and the monk.

Over his shoulder, the monk told them, "I'm Brother Maurice. There are only ten of our order left. Trust none of the others. If asked, you are American tourists—volunteer nothing."

The structure looked simple of line, but enormous. Only three of perhaps fifty windows showed lights. Fallen slates and rotten splinters of wood from the eaves mingled underfoot. Time and weather had had their way with the place for years. A can rattled and something scurried across the courtyard, just out of sight. Muncie's grip tightened on Durell.

Indoors, the air was chill and smelled of mildew.

Brother Maurice lit a kerosene lantern and led them up stairs that had been hollowed by countless pious feet.

They saw no one.

Wet snow pattered against windowpanes.

Brother Maurice showed them through a doorway and Durell clearly saw his death's-head face for the first time. The upthrusting light of the lantern made black hollows in which his eyes glittered; the yellow skin on his cheeks was taut.

"Our guest will remain here," he told Durell as he opened the door to a narrow monk's cell. "This part of the building is vacant. No one will hear, even if he shouts at the top of his lungs. He might as well be dead and buried." The monk lowered his voice to a sinister whisper. "These cells were reserved for the insane in the old days."

There was a narrow plank cot, no mattress, a wooden

stool, a table in the corner, a chamber pot, and a crucifix. That was all.

Caske looked appalled. "Why are you doing this? Do you realize the danger you're putting yourself in? And Mrs. Plettner? I can't be responsible for what my men may do when they catch you." He jabbed with his finger. "Or the courts, if you're lucky enough to be turned over to them. Be sensible! Release me, and I'll pretend none of this happened. All will be forgiven."

Durell spoke with contempt. "Lock him up, Brother Maurice."

"Wait! I—I'm not well." Caske's voice broke. "There isn't even a window."

The monk told him, "Just be glad I didn't chain you in the attic with the rats. There's a place even the brothers won't go."

It was a convincing touch. Durell judged that Caske was ready to do almost anything. He thought he'd try something that had been hatching in the back of his mind. "Let's talk about Dr. Plettner's files," he said.

"I won't sell them to anyone, I promise."

"A promise from a man with your morals is worthless," Durell said bluntly. "Have the files delivered here."

"Here?"

"Tonight."

Muncie looked worried. "How will you know whether they're the real thing? Don't trust him."

"Does it look as if I trust him?"

"Mrs. Plettner! Really! I am a businessman," Caske blustered.

"If you hadn't pressured Peter, none of this would have happened," she told him. "You made him a drunk. You made him run away!"

Durell stepped between them. "I'll release you when you get me those files. Otherwise . . ." He shrugged.

"It's extortion!" Caske blurted.

"Call it what you like."

Caske slumped down onto the cot. "I have no choice, then?"

"Not unless you like solitary confinement—you may have had your last glimpse outside these four walls."

"Don't say that!"

"I'll have to be sure your people don't copy the papers before they deliver them," Durell said. "The only way is not to give them enough time. It took about twenty minutes to drive here. I'll give your man thirty."

"It's not enough," Caske objected.

"If they want you back it is."

Caske shrugged.

Durell said, "Tell him to leave the files by the signpost, but don't tell him you're here. Say you'll be released in Geneva at the Jardin Anglais, after the files have been inspected for authenticity." Durell cut off Caske's protest. "I know, you'll insist on being exchanged directly—and you *will* be waiting at the sign—but I can't let your man know. He might be tempted to bring a dummy file, or none at all. I have to insist."

"Very well," Caske said. "But he may bring dummies, anyhow."

"Not if he thinks your release depends on authenticity. Remember, he's to think you'll be held until that has been established." Durell drew a breath. "He'll bring the real thing," he said. Then, to Brother Maurice, "Where's a phone?"

"This way." He led them back down the stairs and through twin gothic doors embellished with carvings from the Book of Genesis. "My office," he said. "I'm abbot now. It's a long way from French resistance of World War Two days, is it not?"

"How did you end up here?" Muncie asked.

"Ah, she's a curious one," he told Durell. Then, to Muncie, "Suffice it to say, I never dare return to France, my dear lady."

She turned dubious eyes on Durell; he brushed it aside and handed Caske an old-fashioned stand-up telephone.

"You'd better get out of Switzerland, too, after tonight," Caske told the abbot.

A grin crossed the skull-like face. "They are taking me to America, Mr. Caske. Oh? Didn't you think I'd recognize a man of your stature? I haven't been buried out here, you know."

Caske knotted the muscles in his jaw in futile anger. He dialed a number, spoke to someone, and gave him Durell's instructions. When he had finished and put down the phone, he looked past Durell, and his face went white.

Brother Maurice stood a few feet away, covering them all with a German Luger. . . .

Chapter 12

Durell stared at the black muzzle, then the monk's tense face, wondering what the hell had gone wrong.

Caske spoke first. "What's the meaning of this?"

"Put your hands up. All of you," Brother Maurice ordered. "M'sieur Durell, drop your pistol and kick it across the floor to me . . . gently."

"You're biting the hand that feeds you," Durell growled.

"Perhaps it hasn't fed me well enough. Perhaps I shall eat better on my own." The thin voice strengthened with anger. "I've hidden here for thirty-five years, living like an animal in a cage while the rest of the world went by. At last I have the means of escape. This wealthy man can pay me for his freedom—and there's the matter of those files you all seem to value so much. . . ."

Durell tried to explain. "You can't use them; they're full of scientific data—"

"Perhaps someone else can." The Luger swung back and forth nervously.

"But it's not ordinary espionage material—not mere secrets to be put into someone's intelligence mill for a few new facts. They could swing the balance between life and death for thousands of people," Durell pleaded.

"Isn't it always so? And how much is each of those lives worth, do you think? A thousand dollars apiece, perhaps? Could you arrange it for me?"

Durell was overcome with loathing. "You slime . . ."

"Keep your distance, my friend!" There was a charged silence, then the monk said, "Just do as I say. Go back to the cell, the lady first."

They had no choice but to obey.

The air in the cell was frigid. Durell envisioned a mountain of stone surrounding them like a glacier. Muncie was watching him, her eyes wide. He turned away and tried to take stock—he didn't need a hysterical woman's ravings right now. "At least give us a candle," he told Brother Maurice.

"In the drawer of the table," the monk said.

Durell found it and got a light from the lantern. Brother Maurice watched every move with his finger on the trigger.

"You will come with me, M'sieur Caske," the monk said. "Let's go await the files. Then we can talk money."

The door thudded shut. There was a rattle as a key was inserted and the lock was turned.

Muncie beat against the door. "What are you going to do with us?"

The thick door muffled a chilling reply. "I don't have to do anything—time will take care of you for me."

Durell heard a maligning laugh.

Then, silence. . . .

"It could be worse," Durell told Muncie.

"Yeah? How?"

He pointed to the floor. "Rat droppings."

"Ooh!" She shuddered.

"From up there." He pointed at the ceiling. The aged planks were separated by gaps as wide as a quarter-inch in places. He handed his candle to her and moved the stool to the center of the room.

"What are you up to?" she asked.

"We may be able to get through that ceiling," he said. He climbed onto the stool and studied it carefully. "May as well give it a try." He hit the planks with the heel of his hand. Dust sifted down. They didn't come loose, but it felt as if they might, given a little more encouragement.

He dragged the table out of the corner, put the stool on top of that, and climbed up. "Steady the table," he said.

"Sam, I'm not sure I want to get into that ceiling, not if there are rats up there. . . ." She put the candle on the floor; its light made their shadows big on the whitewashed walls.

"It's the only way out," he told her, "rats or not."

"I can't stand rodents."

"You probably won't even see any."

"Probably!"

He banged the ceiling again, harder.

Muncie said, "I thought your monk friend was supposed to be on our side."

"Me, too." He kept hitting the ceiling, hurting his hands.

"The temptation was just too much for him," she said. "Temptation is something I can understand. I had plenty of temptations, traveling all over with Peter. I could've had other men, you know."

Durell took a breather, looking down at her grave blue eyes. "Why didn't you?"

"I've been asking myself that."

Something in her face and in the way she spoke almost made him come down and take her in his arms . . . but if that was what she wanted, she'd picked the wrong time and place. He had to try to stop Brother Maurice. The moment passed, and he went to work on the ceiling once more, beating until he had to clench his jaw in pain.

"I've got a couple of the boards loose," he announced. "Just a minute, now." He finished prying the planks loose.

Dust and rat dung spilled into the cell.

He coughed and covered his mouth. Cold air flooded down over him. "Hand me the candle."

Muncie did as he asked, and he reached overhead and stuck

it on the attic floor, then pulled himself up, shoulders cracking. Muncie got onto the stool, and he lifted her after him.

The attic was an enormous open space where the walls were only shadows in the gloomy distance. Great hand-hewn rafters, stained and split with age, held up the roof; cobwebs hung in clouds. There was no floor, only crossbeams laden with dust and droppings. And there was the furtive rattle of tiny clawed feet. . . .

"Watch your step," Durell cautioned and moved down the building's length, the candle out before him.

Rats squeaked.

The stench of dry rot muddied his nostrils.

He wondered with a sense of urgency how much time had passed since Caske had called for the files. He glanced at his watch: almost twenty minutes. Brother Maurice was sure to grab the files and run—he could take Caske along to ransom later. And once he started running, he could become well-nigh impossible to catch—as the French he'd betrayed during the war had found out.

Not that the files contained everything necessary to manufacture *X. coli*. Information that detailed was only in Dr. Plettner's head, or perhaps in the laboratory destroyed in the fire. But the files could lead to the brink, needing only the biochemical experts and facilities to brew up the killer strain, perhaps within a few days.

It did not cross Durell's mind to doubt that the monk would find a buyer. The world was becoming more insanely violent every day.

The sharp grating sound of gnawing rats' teeth came through the chill air.

They passed a chimney of eroded brick; it was covered with frozen drippings from the roof. Here was a litter of pigeon feathers, bird bones.

Starting at the chimney the attic was floored, but passage was more difficult. There were heaps and stacks of storage, much of it probably forgotten over the ages. The vellum pages of illuminated manuscripts had turned moldy and fallen apart. There were religious paintings emblazoned with gold, icons studded with emeralds and rubies, silver reliquaries, rolled tapestries. And there were ordinary boxes and barrels and mountains of things covered with rugs and sheeting.

"There's a fortune here," Muncie said.

"There must be a door somewhere," he said.

Muncie gripped his arm. "Look!"

He followed her gaze and saw three wooden burial caskets lying just inside the pool of light cast by the candle. "Probably made by the monks for their own," he said.

"It's a bit gruesome, don't you think? To know that your coffin is waiting for you in the attic . . . ?"

"Monks are as much concerned with dying as with living," he replied.

Abruptly he held the candle higher, looking more closely.

"What is it?" she asked, her tone apprehensive. "What do you see?"

Durell's brow creased thoughtfully. "Look at the dust on them—one's got fresh handprints all over it."

"The rats have been gnawing on it, too—look at the edges." Muncie shivered.

They stared at each other, then Durell bent down and found where drops of blood had made mud balls in the dust. Still fresh, it smeared with greasy ease between his thumb and forefinger.

Rats' eyes shone from the near shadows.

Durell looked for Muncie's face.

"I'm frightened," she told him. "Please, let's . . ."

"We can't—not until we find out. . . ."

"Do you think the monk killed Caske? He wouldn't have done that, would he?" She shook her head.

"Maybe. No one would know until they paid a ransom whether Caske was dead or alive." He reached for the lid.

"Are you going to open it?"

"The lid's loose," he told her. He took a breath and pulled the lid up. His face went hard.

The man in the casket was Brother Maurice.

Chapter 13

Brother Maurice was not quite dead.

His skull-face was the color of old ivory, and his lips were skinned back as he strove to breathe. Blood stuck to the chest of his robe where a wet, black bullethole gurgled air. "Help me . . . the rats!" he whispered. "They're coming!" His eyes rolled in terror.

"What happened?" Durell knelt beside the coffin.

"He was . . . too smart." The dying man plucked at Durell and panted for air. "I took too much . . . for granted. Tried to play . . . how you say? . . . big shot." He coughed; the bullethole squirted bloody foam. Feebly, he said, "He's strong . . . and ruthless. . . ."

Durell threw a book at the gleaming eyes creeping out from the darkness. Whether drawn by the smell of fresh blood or a sense of the monk's helplessness, the rats had gotten bolder.

The cold in the unheated attic stabbed at Durell's bones.

"Did he get both guns?" he asked. The monk's eyes rolled back. Durell slapped him. "Did he get both guns!"

"Yes . . . no . . . let me think," he whined.

"You miserable . . . There isn't time to think. I'll leave you to the rats!"

"Please . . .!"

"Sam, for heaven's sakes! Get a doctor," Muncie pleaded.

"Keep out of this," he snarled. "Where's the gun?" he demanded.

Brother Maurice sobbed. "Under . . . cassock . . ."

Feverishly, Durell dug into both pockets. *Under?* He ran his hand down the bloody neck opening of the man's garment and brought the snub-nosed .38 out of an inside pocket.

There was a liquid rattle, and the monk's thin neck arched like a dying bird's. He struggled for air. ". . . rats . . ." He squealed in horror—and died.

Durell had his revolver; that was all that concerned him. "Come on," he told Muncie, but she stood transfixed.

"Don't leave him here," she asked.

Durell sighed wearily and heaved the corpse over his shoulder. It was light enough—Durell suspected the man wouldn't have lived to a ripe old age in any case.

Muncie said: "It's just . . . those rats. I know how he must've felt."

"We didn't owe him anything," Durell said and left it at that.

He felt a draft, and the candle flame sputtered. "There's a door," he said, able to see its bare outlines. As they drew nearer, he saw it was narrow, with forged-iron hardware. He hoped it wasn't locked from the outside.

At that moment, Muncie cried, "Sam! Look at the rats!"

The terror in her voice made his skin crawl. He turned with his burden and saw an arc of glittering eyes pressing closer and closer. There were scores of them. "Get to the door," he barked. "Get out of here."

Before he could say anything else, the rodents attacked in a skittering, screeching rage.

Frantically, he kicked and swatted as they bit his legs and clawed at his trousers, trying to climb him like a tree. He heard Muncie scream in mindless terror. "Stay on your feet!" he yelled, swinging around to help her keep them from pulling her down.

The candle had fallen.

Rats swarmed up, rushing to replace those that Durell kicked and threw across the darkness.

Muncie reeled into him, grabbing at one that had scrambled onto her shoulder. Durell knocked it off and then desperately heaved the body of Brother Maurice into the midst of the blood-lusting rat pack.

There was a sudden, awful rushing of feet as they converged on the corpse and began devouring it voraciously with slavering savagery.

They had left Durell and Muncie for the moment. Muncie wobbled on unsteady legs, then fainted. Sam caught her, cradling her in his arms just as the candle flickered out.

He probed for the door, skin prickling at the tumult behind him. Finding it, he rushed through and slammed it behind him. He sank to the floor with his back against the door, Muncie still in his arms. His heart was pounding. He took a few seconds to pull himself together.

There was no light, not even a window.

He got up on unsteady knees and carried Muncie down a long hallway. His hands were freezing. He found a staircase and descended with cautious steps, pausing at the bottom.

The luminous dial of his wristwatch showed that almost thirty minutes had passed since Caske's call for the files.

Caske would be waiting by the sign.

It would be touch and go whether Durell could get there in time.

There were windows here. He put Muncie on the stone floor beside one and checked her over. As best he could tell, she had no serious injuries. He loosened the upper buttons on her blouse and stung her cheeks with a couple of light slaps. She gave a start.

"It's all right," he told her. "We're out of the attic. No more rats."

She sat up, shivering. "Are you all right?"

"Don't worry about me."

"I'll never be able to sleep again—I know I'll dream . . ." She put her face in her hands.

He pulled her close. "You'll get over it. Believe me?"

"I don't know. Just hold me."

"I've got to go. Stay here and pull yourself together."

"Are you joking?" She leaned away to see his face in the pale light. "I'm not staying in this place!"

"Caske's got a gun—it's dangerous out there," he told her.

She forced a thin smile. "So what else is new?"

He didn't wait for her. If she were coming, she'd have to catch up when she could.

He headed down the snow-powdered drive. The landscape was the color of cigarette ash—and silent, as if it had been buried under a landslide.

He ran through the snow with his gun held ready. He'd kill Caske before he'd let him escape. It would cause a boil of trouble, but that was something he'd worry about at his leisure.

Right now, he had to contend with the possibility of two madmen loose in the world, intent on profiting from the terror of *X. coli.*

The drive was some quarter of a mile long.

What must have been Caske's footprints led the way, a broken line that stretched ahead.

He rounded the last bend in the drive and saw the big frame of Caske, waiting beside the monastery's sign.

Almost too late, he realized that Caske had heard him and raised the Luger. He dived just as the pistol spat fire. Squirming on his belly, he came onto the base of a tree, slid behind it, and triggered a fast shot to keep Caske off balance.

The mountains echoed the gunfire. Then it got very still. He heard his breath.

His frozen fingers ached around the cold steel of the Smith & Wesson.

Caske must have ducked behind the stone columns that held the sign between them. The trickery of the snow's radiance was all Durell had to see by.

"Caske!" he called.

"So, I missed you." Durell thought the arrogant voice came from the direction of the sign, but he couldn't be sure.

"I found the Frenchman," he called.

"Then you know that I'm not to be taken lightly," Caske replied. "I'll kill you, too. If you have any reason left, you'll use your energies to get out of the country and leave me alone."

Durell squinted, trying to see him. "I'd prefer that, but it isn't possible. I have a job to do."

"I'll make a deal with you," Caske called, keeping out of sight.

"No deals," Durell said stubbornly.

"Perhaps we could cooperate. I want Dr. Plettner found as much as you."

"Give up the files."

"But they're my property!"

Anger simmered in Durell—images of the dead he'd seen, revulsion for Caske. *X. coli* was a travesty, an outlaw against nature that no one should own.

He made a dash for another tree to draw fire and pinpoint Caske. There was a shot, and it was a wide miss, coming as he made the shelter of a big fir.

Now he knew for sure that Caske was behind the stone pillars of the sign. He could work his way around him, given the darkness and the snow. He began circling left, from tree to tree, until he had a clear view of the sign.

It came as a jolt to find that Caske had vanished.

He dropped down and looked cautiously about.

A car approached, its headlights making a smear of radiance through the swirling snow, and Durell slid into a roadside ditch, waiting for it to pass.

It slowed.

Maybe it brought the files—or any number of Caske's men.

At least the element of surprise was on his side.

He wondered where Caske was. And what had become of Muncie? She must have heard the gunshots.

The snub-nosed .38 was a hunk of ice in his grip.

From a distance came the rocky rushing sound of the Versoix River.

The car was still slowing, its automatic transmission whining down, disc brakes scraping. . . .

Before it came to a complete stop, Durell jumped from the ditch and yanked the driver's door open, shoving his gun into the driver's face—but it was his own man, Nuri Borodin, K Section's Geneva Control.

"Sam? What . . .?" Nuri was cut short by a gunshot; a slug zipped over Durell's shoulder into the doorpost.

Durell killed the interior light, slamming the door and falling back into the ditch, nerves buzzing.

"Are you all right?" Nuri called as Durell picked his face out of the snow.

"Get out of the car!" he yelled. There was another shot, and he heard the sound of glass splintering in a window.

The car was still barely moving; now it slithered to a halt. The doorlight flashed again as Nuri jumped out, kicked the door closed, and dived for the roadside. He wriggled up the ditch to join Durell, breathing hard.

"What are you doing here?" Durell asked, looking around for Caske.

"You asked me to come, remember?" He sounded angry and winded.

"Damn! I nearly shot you."

"Tell me about it." Nuri held his chest. "I have to get out of this business," he said. "I'm not up to it anymore. Why did you have to kidnap someone like Bernhard Caske?"

"Trust me," Durell said. "He's out here somewhere."

"Caske? *Merde!*"

"Your friend double-crossed us."

"Brother Maurice?"

"He bit off something that choked him—Caske killed him."

"I supposed Maurice would stab us in the back when he thought it would pay enough." Nuri was philosophical. "Sorry it had to be you."

"Apologies accepted."

"What now?"

Durell looked down the highway. A breeze sounded in the trees higher up the mountainside. "He's having Dr. Plettner's file brought out. If we can just get them, nothing else that's happened matters." He shook his head. "But it won't be easy to do with him taking potshots at us. We have to catch him—or silence him."

Nuri drew a flat little .32 automatic from his pocket. His voice was businesslike. "Very well. Shall I go right or left?"

"Take the left. Wait!" He touched Nuri's shoulder. "Isn't that a car parked down there?" He pointed through the darkness. "It just moved up without lights."

"It is," Nuri said.

"They must have tailed you." Durell felt like throwing up his hands.

"What now?"

Durell considered the question as snowflakes fell against his eyes. The smell of pines came through the air. "Let's take whatever time we've got and get Caske—he's the key."

"Look, Cajun!" Nuri pointed toward the approaching headlights of a third car.

"Maybe it's bringing the files," Durell said. "They're to be left by the sign over there. Caske will try to get into the car."

They watched from their cover as the automobile passed the previous one—which had pulled onto the shoulder—and came to a halt beside the stone columns holding the monastery's sign.

The driver got out, leaving the engine running. A brief flash from the car's interior lamp showed a small man in a

111

fedora and overcoat. It was no one Durell knew. In no hurry, he opened a rear door and took out a large box.

"Hugo!" Caske's shout bounced among the rocks and trees.

Durell's head snapped around, eyes searching the shadowy gloom. Nuri started to say something, but Durell silenced him with a wave.

The man called Hugo straightened with surprise. "Herr Caske?"

Caske spoke from hiding, in German. "Wait there, Hugo. Leave the papers inside the car. Don't be afraid."

Durell was caught offguard as Caske showed himself from behind nearby shrubbery. Someone was with him.

"I have the woman," Caske shouted.

"Muncie?" He saw that it was true, even though the night was dark. The small figure could be no one else. Caske's elbow stood out at shoulder height—he was holding his gun on her temple. "Turn her loose. This is between us," Durell called.

"Do you take me for a fool?" Caske moved toward the car, keeping Muncie between himself and Durell. There was no hope of picking him off in this light. "Keep your distance." The words were harsh with desperation.

Nuri whispered to Durell. "We've got to let him go, Cajun."

Durell's feelings were in a turmoil. He was torn between fear of harming Muncie and the overriding necessity of getting Dr. Plettner's material.

Nuri saw his face through the darkness. "Give it up, Cajun," he argued. "That other car is probably loaded with his men, just waiting for us to show ourselves."

Durell heard Muncie cry faintly, her mouth covered by Caske's palm. They were close now, the crunch of their footsteps clearly audible across the snow.

Caske was getting away, and there was nothing he could do to stop him. Durell frowned, his mouth drawing a hard line across his face. "I'll catch up with you again," he called.

"Your bad luck if you do." Caske laughed.

Then, without warning, the mysterious third car that had been waiting on the shoulder roared to life, lurching onto the highway with spinning tires and blazing lights.

Caske gave a surprised yell.

That was when Durell realized Caske was as ignorant of the car as he was. . . .

Chapter 14

With the car zooming toward him, Caske hurled Muncie out of the way and jumped into Hugo's vehicle.

Almost before Durell realized what had happened, Hugo had gunned his car away in a shower of snow and gravel.

The next moment, he and Nuri were lying in the ditch staring after the two automobiles as they raced up the mountain.

Caske was escaping with the files; maybe those chasing him would get them. Durell couldn't allow either to happen. "Let's get after them," he snapped.

Scrambling to his feet, he found Muncie sprawled in the snow and hauled her up. "Get in Nuri's car."

Nuri's experience in Switzerland had made him an expert mountain driver, and they soon drew in sight of the taillights of the other two cars. The narrow road followed every hump and hollow of the terrain as it twisted in and out among the ravines and cliffs. The cars made a chain of thunder and light as they surged higher and higher above snowy fields and vineyards.

"Be careful!" Muncie cried as they slithered around an unbanked curve.

Durell sat braced, half expecting to crash any second.

Nuri peered ahead intently, the light from the dash reflecting on his outthrust jaw. "No matter how many times you drive a road like this in the snow, it's never easy," he said.

"Just don't lose them," Durell told him.

They sped on another mile, the road getting higher and icier every minute. Then, rounding a curve, taillights flared ahead, and sparks and metal flew into the air—the car pursuing Caske had slammed into a roadside cliff. It spun around wildly, scattering parts, tires screeching, then rolled over twice before stopping on its top.

Evading the wreckage somehow, Nuri brought his car to a controlled halt. "My God . . . ." he said.

The wreck had exploded in flames, and the passenger compartment was an inferno. Durell heard someone screaming, but couldn't see him.

He leaped from the car and ran past the fire, gazing through the blowing fog and snow. He could barely make out Caske's receding taillights. Nuri came up beside him. "We'll never get past this mess in time to catch him."

"He's gone, then." Durell sighed bleakly.

The wreck burned furiously, acrid fumes of paint and upholstery whirling through the falling snow. There was a taint of burned flesh in the air.

As they made their way back to their car, Nuri said, "I wonder who they were."

"Maybe we're about to find out," Durell said.

Nuri's eyes followed his gaze to see someone stagger out of the shadows into the fiery light. . . .

His name was Viktor Paramonov, and his papers—given to Durell only at gunpoint—said he was attached to the Soviet consular service agricultural commodity section in Geneva, but Durell knew hundreds of KGB names and Paramonov's was among them.

He was tall and thin, with devil's brows and eyes like a

fox's. Somehow he'd been thrown from the car and come away with nothing worse than a broken arm.

Durell fanned him, withdrawing a Czech-manufactured 7.62 mm Model 52 pistol. Paramonov didn't resist. He sat down in the snow, holding his arm. "Get me a doctor," he said in good English.

"How did you know where to come tonight? Who tipped you off?" Durell demanded.

Paramonov grinned through clenched teeth. "I need medical treatment," he said.

Durell turned to Nuri. "It must have been your phone; the damn phone must have been tapped."

"I don't think so, Cajun." Nuri wore a hurt expression.

"You don't think so, but there's no other explanation." Durell kept his annoyance off his face, but he couldn't hide it in his voice. He turned to the Russian. "You won't tell us, will you, comrade." It was a statement.

"My arm has been seriously injured," Paramonov complained.

"You're lucky. You could be in there, frying with your pals." He pointed to the burning vehicle.

"We only want what you want, Samuel Durell," Paramonov said. "Why sound so angry? I thought you were a professional."

"I'm tired of you getting in my way," Durell said.

"Why don't you make it easy for us, then? There are more of us than there are of you. You will lose in the end in any case."

"Guess I'll just have to try harder," Durell replied.

"Where are you going?" Paramonov cried. "You can't leave an injured man here to freeze!"

"Think of it as another way of thinning the odds against me," Durell told him, getting into Nuri's car.

As Nuri got behind the wheel, Muncie said, "Are you leaving that man here?"

Paramonov was wobbling toward them, his unbroken arm outstretched in the headlights.

"Yes," Durell said. "Let's go!"

* * *

The tables were turned. With Bernhard Caske loose—and probably screaming for the authorities to do something—Durell was the hunted instead of the hunter.

It wasn't wise to go back to the hotel, so Nuri drove him and Muncie to a K Section safe house in the *Vieille Ville*, Geneva's old town. It was an unprepossessing townhouse set in a row of stone facades like slices in a loaf of bread.

Durell phoned the hotel and arranged for Nuri to pick up their luggage and deliver it to lockers in Cointrin Airport. Nuri set off, leaving Durell to soak in a hot bath and wonder what move to make next.

The fact was, he'd run out of possibilities, he decided. After his failure tonight, he felt sure he wouldn't be lucky enough to get his hands on Caske again. The man would be too wary.

Which meant that the Plettner files in Caske's possession were out of reach. He was left with no choice but to strike them off his list and forget about getting any help from Caske's direction.

The best he could hope from Caske was not to be arrested—or, perhaps, murdered—before he could get out of Switzerland.

He was a fugitive here, as of now.

A fugitive from Bernhard Caske's power in the very seat of that power.

Durell sat in the steaming tub, sipping bourbon and feeling the fatigue ooze out of his bones. When he'd had enough, he dried himself and dressed in the same clothing he'd worn all day. He saw the cut in his jacket and was reminded of the man who'd tried to knife him earlier. It seemed ages ago. He shrugged the memory away.

"It's about time," Muncie scolded, taking his place in the bathroom. He'd forgotten about her, although he didn't see how, now that he was somewhat restored. He heard water running. "Umm! It's marvelous!" she called.

He turned on the radio and tuned in Radio Suisse Internationale, the Voice of America and, finally, the BBC, looking for news. There was only a potpourri of music and meaningless talk.

Giving up, he went into the kitchen. He hadn't any appetite—not with the way the day had ended—but he knew he should eat anyway, so he slammed through the cabinets. Fifty cans of soup and no bread. Stale dry cereal. No fresh milk, only powdered. He couldn't abide it.

Grumpy, he made coffee.

There was a standard provisions list for all K Section safe houses, but nobody followed it.

His mind went back to the attempted stabbing. It could take weeks for the trail of his assailant to lead anywhere. Hoping for a break, he'd asked Nuri to notify Interpol of American interest in the man's movements over the past forty-eight hours.

He knew his best hope for a fresh start lay with Ronald and Tina Durso. They must have taken the photo he'd found on the assassin.

It must be that one or both of them were scheming with Plettner.

Another of Nuri's tasks this evening would be to inquire discreetly of his sources in the Swiss police and intelligence communities as to the whereabouts of the American couple.

Durell had just taken a sip of his first cup of coffee, wishing for the chicory-laced brew he kept in his Washington apartment, when Nuri called. "Good news, Cajun."

"Impossible."

"The lady named Tina Durso? She's left a message for you at the hotel."

"What did she say?"

"She has to talk to you. Very important. She's at the Hotel Salève. It's on Quai Gustave-Ador, near the jet fountain. Know it?"

"What's her room number?"

"Two twenty-two. Look out for a trap, Cajun."

"That's probably what it is." Durell's tone was matter-of-fact.

"Want me to come and back you up?"

"You have other things to do."

When Durell hung up, he turned and saw Muncie watching

him with worried eyes. She was wrapped in a towel, beads of bath water standing on her shoulders. "Was that Nuri?" she asked.

Durell nodded, coming from the kitchen. He took his tie from the bedpost and knotted it neatly around his neck.

She hadn't moved. "Well?"

"Tina wants to see me," he told her.

"Don't go," she said. "Please."

"I don't really have any choice," he said.

"Send the police!"

"You seem to forget that if I called the police, they'd come for me, not her. You'd end up in jail, too." He opened a closet and took out his hat and overcoat. He didn't hear her bare feet cross the room, but somehow he felt her come up behind him. "Don't you ever stop taking chances?" she asked.

He turned and found her dusky eyes pleading with him. He gave himself a pleasant second to take her all in, from the autumn browns of her hair to the skimpy towel and good legs, then back again. "I'm not the only one taking chances," he said, wanting to reach for her.

"Stay," she breathed. "For me?" He decided she meant that literally, but before he could answer, she let the towel drop.

Her skin glowed from the steamy bath.

She was beautiful, compelling. As she held her arms out to him, the taut globes of her breasts lifted, beckoning. . . .

He decided half an hour couldn't make that much difference to the end of the world.

Just as he reached for her there was a knock on the door.

"Damn!" she exclaimed, crossing her arms. She kissed him quickly, promising him with her eyes, and ducked into the bathroom. He hung her towel over the back of a chair, relieved that temptation had been taken away.

Yet he could hardly relax—no one but Nuri was supposed to know where he was. . . .

Chapter 15

Durell stood to one side of the door, back against the wall, gun in his hand. "Who is it?"

"Wilson, Greg Wilson. From the consulate." The words held a furtive urgency. "Let me in."

Durell didn't know any Greg Wilson, but he didn't keep up with the consulate personnel. He turned out the light, then unlatched the door and swung it inward, staying against the wall. "Come in," he said.

Wilson came inside, light from the street flooding in with him. "Stop there. Don't move." Durell saw that he was dressed in a blue suit of continental cut. Moving behind him, he frisked him. No gun.

"Oh, for Christ's sake, stop playing games," Wilson sneered.

"I leave the games up to the diplomats. Your ID," Durell growled.

The man handed him a wallet. Durell motioned with his gun." Close the door. Turn on the lights." Wilson found the light switch beside the door. He looked about thirty, with short red hair and the smug superiority of a career foreign-office type. Durell studied his papers.

"You're the cause of considerable embarrassment, Mr. Durell," Wilson said.

"No doubt." Durell returned the wallet.

"Fortunately, the Swiss government will allow us to send you back to the United States—fortunately for you and for us."

"Us?"

"We in the diplomatic corps represent the U.S. government abroad. We have a certain image to maintain, and *you* are persona non grata."

"How did you know the location of this safe house?" Durell asked.

Wilson blinked. "I don't have to answer to you, sir."

Durell persisted. "This is a K Section safe house: State Department personnel aren't privy to such information."

"Does it really matter? You're an outlaw. How dare you point to rules and regulations!" Wilson made an impatient gesture. "Put on your hat, and let's go."

Durell didn't move. He was thinking: Wilson wouldn't have been able to get in touch with Nuri—Nuri had been too busy since they'd returned from the monastery. And if Nuri had been prevailed upon to reveal the location, why would Wilson want to hide his source?

What had obviously happened was that Caske had yelled loudly enough to be heard in Washington, and somebody there had sold Durell out.

Not General McFee, though.

If his boss had wanted him to terminate his mission, he'd have contacted Durell at the safe house by now and withdrawn his Q clearance.

But he hadn't.

McFee meant for him to proceed as he saw fit, and that was all that mattered.

Durell lifted his gun. "Sit down," he snapped.

"Now, see here—"

"Shut up. Muncie!"

She came out of the bathroom, fastening a last button, her eyes intimate in their brief glance at Durell. She didn't seem to know what to say to the irate diplomat.

"Bring us a bed sheet," Durell told her. "We have to tie him up."

"Are you sure we should?" she asked.

"You can't do that!" Wilson cried.

"Just get the sheet."

The look in Durell's eyes dampened Wilson's combativeness; his voice took on a more reasoning tone. "Mr. Durell, you're going to get yourself into an awful mess of trouble. I *am* expected back at the consulate, you know." He looked down the gun barrel and licked his lips.

When Muncie returned he told her to hold the gun. He took the sheet and tore it into strips.

"This is really outrageous, you know that?" Wilson fumed as Durell tied him to a chair. "All we want is to save you from prosecution by Swiss authorities."

Durell tightened the last knot and stood back.

"If you want to help, stay out of my way," he said. He cracked the door and regarded the snowy street. It was almost deserted; the hour was late.

"You're not going to leave me here like this?" Wilson protested.

Durell nodded toward Muncie. "She'll be here—and she's good company."

"One last time—don't go," she said.

"I'll be back as soon as I can. You're not to worry. Lock the door and don't answer it for anyone but Nuri."

Then he went into the night. . . .

Durell left his taxi a block from the Hotel Salève and went inside through a service entrance that smelled faintly of food and steam tables. He got to the second floor by a back staircase.

The hotel was old and elegant, its genteel corridors hushed as midnight approached.

He knew the risk he was taking. Only three persons could have photographed him on Plettner's island, and he didn't think Muncie had done it. That left only two: Ronald or Tina or both.

Even if this were a trap, it would be a step forward. All he had to do was survive, and he'd know who he was after. Sometimes he wondered how he could think of his survival so coolly, but it was old habit by now, no emotion to it. The almost certain knowledge that someday he wouldn't survive didn't make him feel much either. He'd lived with it too long.

He approached the room cautiously.

The corridor was decorated with several Chinese vases and glided plaster moldings. Subdued street lighting shone through an arched window that filled the end of the hall. Waves of reflection came through it from moving headlights, winking signs.

He tapped on Tina's door. ''Mrs. Durso?''

No response.

He knocked again, not loudly. He thought he might have heard something inside, but couldn't have said what. A tautness gathered in his middle.

He inspected the door for anything that might trigger a boobytrap and, finding nothing, tried the knob. It wasn't locked. ''Mrs. Durso!'' He stared at the door, helpless to know what was on the other side. He had a hunch someone was in there.

With a look up and down the hallway, he took out his pistol, turned the doorknob, and pushed the door inward half an inch, just enough so the bolt couldn't spring back into its receptacle.

Moving back a step, he raised his foot and slammed it against the door, knocking it open with a clatter, seeing a darkened room.

A woman screamed.

He leaped into the darkness hearing an evil cough, his mind yelling *silencer!* as he scrambled for cover.

Another coughing report and a vase exploded at his shoulder.

He couldn't return the fire; he didn't know where Tina was.

Pain seared across his forearm.

The man was shooting quickly, indiscriminately.

Tina cried out, sobbing incoherently as Durell ducked and dodged, scrambling through the darkness for his life. The darkness was friend and foe. He dumped a table, heard a slug thump into the wood.

He was puzzled by a dull thud, overlaid by the *ding* of a telephone bell . . . a muffled cry of pain. Then he heard the phone crash against the floor.

"I got him, Mr. Durell. Help!"

Tina had cracked the man across the head with the telephone. Durell heard them scuffling and he lunged into the reeling frame of his assailant, knocking Tina aside and grappling for his gun. They went down groping blindly, unsure where the gun lay. A fist hit Durell, sending lights flashing through his head, and then he was on his back, the heavy weight of the other man crushing into him. A grip of iron clamped onto his throat. He heard his own breath as if from a distance, like an animal in a trap.

The blackness of the room seemed to be creeping behind his eyes.

Desperately he swung at the man's kidneys, heard a yelp of pained surprise, and threw him off.

Tina flipped on the lights as they scrambled to their feet, and he found himself staring at someone who for some barely remembered reason was startlingly familiar. He had high cheekbones and dark almond eyes, thick wavy hair, a cleft chin and mustache. Something unconcealed in the eyes betrayed mad dreams; they were as merciless as an attack dog's.

He fitted Miss Nydia Duka's description of the man who'd vaccinated her in San Juan, and who must have planted the *X. coli* aboard the *Sun Rover*.

"You're Luis Alegra!" Durell said.

Tina spoke up. "Don't move!" She'd found the silencer-equipped Colt that Alegra had dropped, and she had it aimed at the Puerto Rican.

124

Alegra moved with astonishing speed, darting for the door. Tina fired but missed. Alegra threw a lamp table at her and knocked her down.

Durell made a grab for him, but he had the advantage by a step and dashed out of the room.

Durell chased him into the corridor in time to see him dive through the enormous arched window at the end. He ran there and looked through: Alegra was sliding off a canopy over the hotel entrance, taking a cascade of powdery snow down with him.

Durell, realizing there was no hope of catching him, watched him vanish into the night.

He drew back from the broken window, avoiding the faces of startled onlookers on the street below. He dared not draw any attention to himself—if he could help it.

"Monsieur? Shall I call the police?" The speaker was a short, dark Frenchman who peered from his hotel room. Other doors were opening.

Durell straightened his lapels and spoke gravely. "I think not, monsieur. The matter involves an affair of the heart."

"Ah! Of course. I thought, perhaps, a burglar . . ."

"*Non*. Only one who would steal a wife's affections," Durell replied with assumed gallantry. "I will compensate the hotel for damages. *Bonne nuit*."

Durell did not smile as the door closed respectfully. He returned to Tina and held out a hand, helping her to her feet. "You all right?"

"I guess. Thanks." Her red hair was disheveled, and she had a bruise on her cheek. "Luis Alegra, huh? How'd you know his name?"

Durell pocketed the man's gun. "It's a long story," he said. He led her to the sofa. "Sit down."

"No need, really." She smiled warmly. "Your arm's bleeding. Be back in a sec." She brought a hot washcloth and bathed the flesh wound as they talked.

"When I told Ron I'd asked you to come, he blew his stack. I don't really know why. He called this, this Luis Alegra to wait for you here. There wasn't a thing I could do about it, honestly. And when you knocked, he put his hand over my mouth.''

"If you hadn't hit him with the phone, I might be dead now,'' Durell told her.

She looked frightened and despondent. "But he got away. I'm so scared he'll come back!'' She wiped a tear from the corner of an eye. "And I'm really scared for Dr. Plettner, Mr. Durell. I . . . I really love him—oh, I know you must think I'm awful, but . . .'' She put her face in her hands. "What's happening?'' she sobbed. "What are people like that man, Luis Alegra, after? And those men who came to the island?''

"Your husband's in it, too,'' Durell said. "Otherwise he wouldn't have sent Alegra here tonight. Has he told you anything? Given you any hints?''

"No.'' She shook her head. "Nothing, Mr. Durell.''

"Very well. But you called me here for something—something that got him very upset. . . .''

"I guess it did, but I knew you were looking for Dr. Plettner, and I didn't see any harm in it.''

"In what?'' He held her gaze.

"In telling you there's a man who works for Mr. Caske—I guess word must've got around today about you—he wanted you to come to his place tonight. He told me he's Dr. Plettner's best friend.''

"Best friend?'' Durell was shocked to hear that the scientist had a best friend in Geneva and Muncie hadn't told him.

Tina went on. "He said he's worried about Dr. Plettner. He thinks Peter'd be better off if you found him.''

Durell couldn't believe what he was hearing. "This man knows where Dr. Plettner is?'' he asked.

"He said he did,'' she replied.

Durell gripped her shoulders. "Tell me where I'm to meet him,'' he said urgently.

Theodore Biner lived in Geneva's Bohemian sister city, Carouge, on the south side of the Arve River. His apartment was above a blue-painted shop with a steep roof of mountain slate. Paintings of the Matterhorn, clocks, and china bric-a-brac in the shop window were visible by the radiance of old wrought-iron street lamps.

Durell paused as he approached, because he saw a knot of people standing on the sidewalk talking in hushed, excited tones. Then he went on, filled with dread.

From a distance came the sound of a police car or ambulance.

The dread grew: He'd guessed that Durso meant to get to Biner first. He should have known that Durso also intended to silence him.

On the island, Durso had made a pretense of wanting Durell to find Dr. Plettner—but that had been a cover, a smokescreen—and the man certainly had been careful not to give Durell any concrete assistance.

Now that Durso seemed to be in league with Plettner, it was obvious he'd try to seal Biner's lips to keep Plettner's whereabouts from Durell.

A question that nagged at him was why Muncie hadn't taken him to Biner. Surely she'd know a man who claimed to be her husband's best friend.

Ignoring the bystanders, he entered the building and ascended a cramped staircase. Two women, both dressed in cheap, heavy sweaters and shawls, probably Biner's neighbors, stood on the small landing. They looked worriedly at him and seemed unable to decide whether they should challenge him.

He went past them and found Biner, just as he'd feared.

Biner was nearly dead.

He lay in the middle of a cluttered room in a pool of darkening blood. Durell rolled him over as the women watched, and found two bulletholes in the chest of the silk dressing gown.

The police car was drawing close.

A faucet dripped.

"Biner!" Durell shook the man.

The dazed eyes fluttered weakly.

"I'm Samuel Durell. You told Mrs. Durso you wanted to see me."

The eyes closed.

Durell bent close. "Where's Dr. Plettner?"

A bloody hand lifted with effort, as if to fend him off.

"Tell me!" Durell shook him again. There wasn't much time left.

Once more the gray eyes glittered in the pale face. Biner's lips worked to speak. Durell waited, willing the man to tell him. The police were nearly outside the building entrance. He looked about and located a window that would open onto the back side of the building. There was an alley there.

Biner was trying to say something. . . .

"What?" Durell lifted his head close to Biner's face, wanting to force the words out.

"M . . . Mother . . . Mary . . ."

Biner went limp. Durell knew he was finished, but he couldn't accept it. Was this it: Mother Mary?

"Who's Mother Mary!" he shouted at Biner. But he was shouting at a dead man.

A restraining hand gripped his shoulder, and he remembered he wasn't alone. It was one of the women. "Stop that!" she scolded. "Who are you? What are you doing here?"

Durell heard the police car pull up outside. He hurried to the window and opened it. Below was a roof covered by deep snow and, beyond, the black abyss that was a twisting alley.

"*Arrêtez!* Police, police!" the woman yelled.

He crawled through the opening, sinking up to his knees in snow. The sky was the color of hot coals where clouds reflected the city's lights.

A frigid breeze whipped grains of snow against his eyes and cheeks.

The snow-covered roof was dangerously slippery, but he was in a hurry—he had to get back to Tina. He could wait for Durso there.

The slap of running feet came to him. Cops were rounding the corner into the alley—he was cut off with nowhere to go.

He tried to go faster but his feet zipped out from under him and he sat down hard. Suddenly he was sliding with the whole snowpack toward the edge of the roof. The next second he shot into the air.

Disoriented and out of control, all he could do was brace himself. Amid the jumble of alarmed thoughts that raced through his mind in the second before impact, the fear of being injured did not stand out, but the regret he'd feel at being caught by the Swiss police.

Then something slammed into his back.

And there was nothing. . . .

Chapter 16

Durell was freezing.

The arm that Alegra's bullet had creased throbbed and stung.

He thought he was back at the monastery, where he'd been entombed in an icy dungeon.

He was fighting off rats, but he knew no matter how many he killed there would be more, and when he fell down exhausted—as sooner or later he must—they would eat him alive.

He dreamed that his arm hurt because one of them had gotten a hold of it with its teeth. He couldn't shake it loose.

He heard voices, realized it was Caske and Brother Maurice, watching and laughing.

Helpless rage cut at him like jagged glass.

The rats bore him down and were overwhelming him. He felt their teeth cutting into his neck, chewing his muscle, but there were so many of them he couldn't move. Their snouts were inside his gut, disemboweling him.

He couldn't breathe . . . suffocating!

He cried out!

"Merde! Où est-il, donc?"

Who was speaking French? Durell came to his senses groggily. His head ached. He started to rub it, but his arm was hard to move, as if he were wrapped in a blanket—or buried. He gave up and lay there, his mind reeling. His mouth was full of something cold. He spat. He could see nothing.

Footsteps squeaked on cold snow nearby.

He felt he would freeze to death. His face was covered with snow. He listened and didn't move. More voices came to him in muffled French—the police!

"I'm certain he came out through that window."

"Well, he got away. We've lost him."

"He must've had wings. Who could he have been? Surely not the murderer."

"Of course not. But why would he run? He knew something he didn't want us to know. . . ."

The footsteps receded. They were leaving.

Durell shivered uncontrollably. Now he understood what had happened: The fall had knocked him out, and snow he'd dislodged from the roof had buried him in a minor avalanche.

He didn't know how long he'd been unconscious.

He waited a while longer, gritting his teeth. He had enough air to breath; the snow was loose. His face burned and his fingers ached, their tips numb.

He stayed where he was.

He heard nothing more, and still he waited. He had no way of knowing where the police were, or who might see him when he got up. But he dared not stay there too long, or he would freeze.

If he hadn't tried to force Bernhard Caske's hand, the police wouldn't be after him. He could have told them he was one of Biner's friends, or a relative. But he'd had to do what he'd done to Caske; he'd been compelled to seek whatever advantage he could against the doomsday threat that only he and a handful of others knew about.

The threat could become a horrible reality at any time . . . tomorrow . . . tonight!

He wriggled out of the snowbank, got onto his knees, and peered up and down the alley. The shadows seemed empty. Looking over his shoulder, he saw the window from which he had escaped. A head wearing a policeman's cap moved across the light.

He brushed the snow out of his face, got his breath, stole quietly away.

His head hurt and his arm burned. He walked fast, trying to warm himself as he looked for a taxi. He was a fugitive from the Swiss and his own countrymen, but at least he'd got something for his efforts.

Mother Mary. If only he understood its significance.

What did it mean?

Of all that Biner might have told him, he'd chosen that . . . in the midst of the trauma of dying.

Had he been delirious? Did it mean anything at all?

What if he'd only been praying? Durell stopped in his tracks, appalled. What if Biner had taken his dying breath to call on the Virgin Mary!

He shook his head and continued to the Hotel Salève, where he hoped to find Ronald Durso, now that he knew which side Durso was on.

This time he didn't knock—but he found the door locked. From a small leather case he kept in his jacket pocket he selected a steel pick, inserted it in the keyhole and twisted the knob, pushing the door slowly open. He took out his gun and went in.

The room was a mess: The shattered vase was still scattered on the floor; the lamp table lay where Alegra had thrown it. Angry bullet holes stitched the wall and a sofa.

Durell touched the wound stiffening on his arm and grimaced. He pushed up his sleeve and checked it. He'd had worse.

They were gone. He knew it before he even looked in the closet. Sure enough, it was empty.

They had cleaned up their things and cleared out, Tina willingly or unwillingly.

He cursed, put away his revolver, and cursed again.

If *Mother Mary* meant anything, maybe Muncie would know. She was his last hope.

"Sam! He got away!" It was the first thing Muncie said.

"Wilson? How?"

Her eyes were apologetic. "The sheet must've been rotten. Look, he tore it right in two. I feel so stupid and useless."

"You couldn't have stopped him," he told her.

"He just walked out. Laughed at me!"

"He'll be back. How long ago?" He looked out the window.

"Five minutes, maybe ten. I don't know." She wrung her hands. "I'm sorry."

"Get your things," he said. He was in a hurry to leave.

"I didn't know whether to stay here or not, but I knew if I didn't, you wouldn't know where to find me." She pulled on her coat.

"Let's go," he said. He glanced outside. "Uh-oh. He's back with the troops."

A black Mercedes had parked at the curb.

"Are you sure that's him?" She was looking over his shoulder.

"Who else?" Durell suddenly felt very tired. Muncie looked at him with wide eyes, waiting to be told what to do. What could he say—run? They'd have her before she'd gone a block—she was too slow, too awkward in her high heels—and there was no place to hide.

He'd have to run and leave her. She'd spend a long time in jail—the U.S. government wouldn't help her. But his mission came before any personal consideration.

"Muncie . . ." he began.

"Go ahead, Sam. Get out while you can." She'd known what he was thinking.

He started to kiss her, but the noise of a car door closing drew his eyes outside again. His mouth tensed, and his hand went under his coat, bringing out the .38.

"Sam, you can't use that on your own people!" Muncie said.

"Stay back from the door."

"Isn't it Wilson?"

"It's him, all right—but I don't think he's with friends." Wilson was between two men, being half dragged toward the front door. His head hung drunkenly from his shoulders.

Durell heard Russian spoken.

"He's run afoul of the KGB," Durell growled. "The sonofabitch told them where the safe house is."

Muncie gasped. "What are we going to do?"

Before Durell could reply, there was a knock at the door. Speaking in English, a man called, "Mrs. Plettner? Open the door, please. We're friends of Mr. Durell. He's had an accident."

"They called him Mr. Durell," Muncie said in bewilderment.

"Looks like somebody's mixed up. Play along," he told her. He signaled for her to open the door, but she shook her head in fright.

"Please let us in—you can trust us. Mr. Durell is seriously injured." Then, in a hushed tone, Durell heard Russian spoken again. "Shall I force the door?"

"*Nyet*, you fool, you want to wake up the entire street?"

There was another knock, and Durell crossed to Muncie, pushing her to the door and turning the latch for her. He stepped back out of the way. "Speak to them," he urged.

Nervously, she said, "Come in."

The door swung back, covering him. He felt a draft of icy air and heard the same voice. "So! Mrs. Plettner?"

"Yes. What happened?" He couldn't see her. There came the shuffle of the Russians coming through the door, then the door swung back to close, showing two of them with their backs to him. One was holding Wilson up.

"I'm afraid," one of them said, "that it was necessary for us to—how shall I say it?—*convince* Mr. Durell here of the necessity for telling us where to find you, Mrs. Plettner."

"You beat him?" She sounded horrified.

"Had we known you were here when we picked him up on the street outside, it would have saved us considerable trouble—and him considerable pain. Forgive me. We are of the *Komitet*

Gosudarstvennov Bezopasnosti.'' He made a stiff little bow. ''Do not be frightened. We have come to take you under Soviet protection.''

Muncie glanced helplessly toward Durell. The Russian saw it and started to turn. ''Don't move,'' Durell snapped, but the man reached for a gun, perhaps betting that Durell would be indecisive.

He lost.

The roar of Durell's gun shocked the ears in the confinement of the room. He felt the buck of the revolver and saw the Russian jerk up on his toes at the same instant. Everything seemed to stop for a lucid moment and he saw the man's hard, sharp-beaked face, like that of a turtle, the jaw dropping with a hiss as the bullet splintered breastbone and shattered the heart.

The other agent released his grip on Wilson and spun toward Durell half a beat after the first, reaching behind him toward a belt holster. His face had the unhealthy blue pallor that spoke of bad lungs or a heart condition, and yellow tar coated his teeth as lips skinned back in a snarl.

Durell squeezed the trigger a second time.

The KGB man's hateful eyes bulged with shock as the impacting slug smacked him over the left eyebrow and the back of his skull burst, spraying pink fluid and tissue.

A sound of revulsion came from deep in Muncie's throat. Her tweed suit was splattered with gore.

Wilson lay on the floor looking around in a daze. His face was a mask of welts and bruises, his swollen lips crusted with blood, eyes nearly closed.

Durell remembered a third Russian when he heard the sound of glass breaking at the rear door.

He skipped to the kitchen entrance, from which he saw the man's gloved hand reach through a broken pane and fumble with the latch. The Russian saw him, too—another pane spat shards of glass as snapped off a shot that missed.

Durell fired quickly, drilling the door, and saw a dark form slide down the glass and out of sight.

The gloved hand went limp in the broken pane, snagged above the doorknob.

Durell soaked a towel in hot water and sponged off Wilson's face. He heard Muncie running water in the bathroom. "Wilson? Do you know who I am?"

Wilson hesitated. "Durell?"

"What happened?" He propped him up, still toweling the cuts and bruises.

"They thought I was you," Wilson mumbled.

"Why?"

"Nuri—he told them where the safe house was. They were looking . . . for Mrs. Plettner. Knew she was with you somewhere."

Durell was dubious. "Nuri wouldn't tell them—where is he?"

Wilson nodded feebly. "He told them. They made him. Picked him up after following him from your hotel. They'd staked it out . . . looking for you." He took a couple of long breaths. "They bragged about it to me—killed him and threw him in the lake. They said they'd do the same to me."

Durell threw the towel down, feeling sick and sad. Nuri had been a survivor; he'd thought Nuri would make it to retirement.

Wilson continued, his voice edged with pain. "They wouldn't believe I wasn't you," he said. "They got here just as I was walking away. They threw me into the car and took me someplace . . . and beat me until I told them what they wanted to know. Really worked me over—I couldn't take any more of that. I told them where to find Mrs. Plettner."

"Calm down. We'll get you medical attention. Muncie?" Durell guessed that a couple of minutes had passed since all the shooting. He reloaded his revolver, waiting for Muncie to come.

Her face was waxen beneath the tumbled curls of her hair, and there was an expression of self-imposed calm on her mouth. Her eyes shone like glass against the frosty pale of her skin. Patches of dark dampness splotched the places where she'd tried to clean her clothing.

He said, "They thought Wilson was me, because they caught him coming out of here—Nuri told them this was the safe house."

She looked worried. "Is he—?"

"There's nothing we can do for him." Durell lowered his voice. "Put it out of your mind."

"Is that so easy for you to do?" There was subdued anger in her reply.

"We'd better get out of here before the police come," he told her. "We'll drop Wilson off at the Cantonal Hospital." He lifted Wilson, helping him off the floor.

"Ow! My shoulder!" Wilson whined.

Durell helped him down the steps to the Russian's Mercedes. "Did they leave the keys in it?" he asked Muncie.

She checked. "We're in luck," she said.

He helped Wilson into the car. He could smell coal smoke in the crisp air, and the cold sunk icy teeth into his nose. No sign of police. Maybe the shots hadn't been heard. He glanced at his wristwatch. It was ten after two, dead of night. None of the windows in adjacent buildings had been turned on.

As they drove away, Wilson, sitting between him and Muncie, said, "You're still out of line, Durell."

He made no reply, concentrating instead on driving through the snowy streets.

"You'll never get out of the country," Wilson said. "If you don't surrender to the consulate, Caske and the Swiss will have you for lunch."

Durell said, "Didn't tonight tell you anything?"

"Like what?"

"There's more to this than Caske's hurt feelings."

"All I know is I was told to bring you back to the consulate several hours ago, and I still haven't gone there with you. But I'm still trying."

Muncie spoke up. "He saved your life."

"I'm just following orders," Wilson said.

Durell snorted, his eyes on the road. "A true bureaucrat. You'll go far, Wilson."

"What else should I do?"

Muncie said: "You could try to help us."

"The two of you have embarrassed your country," Wilson said. "I wouldn't have been beat up in the first place, if it hadn't been for you." He sounded self-righteous.

They had arrived at the emergency entrance. White light shone through glass doors; a nurse walked past. "Let Mr. Wilson out, Muncie," Durell said.

She got out and held the door of the car open, her breath shining in puffs.

Wilson said, "This is your last chance, Durell. If you don't return to the consulate, you're in real big trouble."

Durell put his hand against the man's shoulder and straightened his arm sharply, tumbling him out. "Goodbye, Wilson," he said.

The last he saw as he drove away with Muncie, Wilson was reeling toward the emergency exit, holding his side. . . .

Chapter 17

"He had a point," Muncie said.

"He was a pain in the ass," Durell replied.

A brief smile played at the corners of her lips. "How *are* we going to get out of Switzerland without getting caught?" she asked.

"Just as important, where are we going?" Durell countered. He glanced into the rearview mirror.

"Back to America? What else can we do?"

Durell let it drop for the moment. He drove on, passing Renaissance-style buildings and a bluff that overlooked the university. They entered the picture-book Grand Rue, where buildings still remained that might have been visited by Calvin or Jean-Jacques Rousseau. Turning left, he followed a dark side street where cobblestones made the Mercedes wriggle comfortably, like a fat man having his back scratched.

He parked in front of a shuttered shop. A sign shaped like a clock hung over the entrance. The sidewalk was empty; the snow showed no footprints. In the street, two, maybe three cars had left curving trails since the snow had begun piling up.

Muncie came closely behind him as he climbed steps to the door and picked the lock.

Inside, he did not turn on the lights. He'd been here before. There was a narrow hallway with a W.C. on the left, stairs on the right, a closed door at the end. He stumbled over a pile of boxes, making his way to the door. Muncie was quiet, as if afraid someone would hear them. "Nuri lived alone," he told her.

"So this is Nuri's shop," she said.

He got her through the door, closed it, then turned on a light. They were in a windowless space that led to descending stairs. "What are you going to do?" she wondered.

"You'll see," he told her. The cellar was stuffed with every kind of clock, all of them ticking at once. He turned on a fluorescent light. It flickered and hummed over a messy workbench covered with the clutter of a watchmaker's trade.

He sat on the edge of the workbench and faced Muncie. "I need your help," he said.

"I've tried . . ."

He waved for silence. "I don't have to tell you again how important it is that I find Dr. Plettner, do I?"

"What's the matter?" she asked. "What did Tina tell you?"

"She sent me to Theodore Biner. Ever hear of him?"

Muncie looked away nervously. "I—I may have. I don't know. . . ."

"That's strange," Durell said, "because he told Tina he was one of your husband's best friends."

"Why are you looking at me that way? Why have you changed?"

"Because I found you haven't been leveling with me, and I don't know what to do about it." He looked at her with solemn eyes. "I need your help—you may be my last hope."

"I've been helping," she protested.

"But now you claim not to know a man who's a close

friend of your husband.'' Durell crossed his legs, holding a knee and staring at her.

Her pretty chin jutted out. "If he's such a good friend, what did he want with you?"

"Did Dr. Plettner know anybody named Mother Mary? Do you?"

"No," she said flatly.

She wasn't even thinking, he could see that. She'd answered too fast.

She said: "If Mr. Biner mentioned such a person, why didn't he tell you more?"

"He's dead. Killed this evening."

Her hand covered her mouth. "Oh, my God!"

"So you did know him." Durell shook her. "Why didn't you tell me about him?" He had an urge to slap her, but he swallowed his anger. "Talk!" he growled.

Tears ran down her cheeks. "Okay!" She sobbed. "Oh, Sam, Ted—Mr. Biner—was supposed to be our go-between, so no one could trace Peter's mail."

Durell flung her away. It was all he could do to keep from punching her. She banged into the wall and turned her face to it, sobbing. "You knew where your husband was all along. That's why you played down his disappearance from the start. You've been shielding him and making a fool of me." His tone became menacing. "You must know what he's guilty of, then."

"He isn't guilty of anything." She raised her voice. "I don't know what's going on. I don't know what happened to start all of this, but he hasn't done anything wrong."

"Stop protecting him, Muncie," he threatened.

"I really don't love him, if that's what you're thinking."

"That's immaterial. I'm waiting to hear where he's hiding." His face was hard, his tone unbending.

"Listen, our marriage was a laugh, and then there was the pressure from Caske. Peter said he just couldn't take it anymore, he had to do something. I thought he'd break off with Caske; it never occurred to me he'd do something like what he did." Her eyes looked for his understanding. "He gave me no warning . . . but he did leave a note. I burned it—there wasn't much in it. He said where he'd gone and begged me not to tell. He said Ted Biner would be his go-between if I had to get in touch. But he *didn't* say where he was going. Didn't trust me that much, I guess. But . . . now I know.''

"Because of Mother Mary?"

She nodded reluctantly.

"Well?"

"Mother Mary is Peter's sister. She's a nun. . . ."

"A mother superior?"

"Yes." Muncie hesitated. "She heads a nursing order in Calcutta."

Sweet relief flowed through Durell. Muncie hadn't failed him, and he'd been so close to failure.

She was speaking. "I went there once for a visit. She's Peter's only close relative, and she works in a mission for the poorest of the poor." She shuddered at the memory. "It was awful." She came closer and looked up into Durell's eyes. "Peter didn't go away to make mischief, Sam. He went for time to think, for renewal. Don't you see?"

"Did he explain that?" Durell asked, his face stern.

"No, but—"

"Then your guess is no better than mine. Remember, Durso killed Biner, apparently to keep Plettner's whereabouts a secret. He wouldn't do that to protect a spiritual holiday."

"Ron killed him?" She was aghast.

"Most likely." Durell crossed to a grandfather clock in a heavy oak case. He felt down the sides.

"What about Caske, then?"

"Durso could have something going with Dr. Plettner— maybe it doesn't include Caske." He felt a bulge, pressed it with a finger and pulled the clock away from the wall on silent hinges, revealing a safe. He didn't know the station combination to the safe, but he didn't need to. A three-digit combination acted like a master key to such safes in Control stations all over the world, and he was one of no more than half a dozen men who knew those three digits.

Opening the safe, he reached past code books and a file of secret communications, and withdrew a metal box.

"What's that?" Muncie asked.

"Phony passports, among other things. Here." He handed her one. "Dream up a name and type it in, along with your vital statistics."

"What about a photo?" she asked.

"We have a Polaroid camera."

"It's so simple. Are you taking me to Calcutta with you?"

"You know where the mission is. It'll save me time."

A thoughtful sadness clouded her gaze. "I feel like I'm betraying Peter, taking you there."

"Look at it this way," he said, "you're betraying lots more if you don't."

Chapter 18

The green landscape below was pocked and lined with ponds and canals as Durell's Boeing jetliner made its final approach to Calcutta's Dum Dum Airport.

Then there came the haze of a city, gleaming oil tanks and ships at anchor on a brown river. Another turn revealed new green, with palm trees and bullock carts and a white church steeple as English as Suffolk sticking up out of the jungle.

The giant aircraft bumped down on a runway.

Muncie turned to Durell. "I hope I'm doing the right thing. What would you have done, if I hadn't told you where to come?"

"You would have told me." His reply was as simple as he could make it.

They paused in the busy terminal long enough for him to make a phone call, then boarded a taxi driven by a turbaned Sikh.

No one seemed to have been waiting for them.

A pall of industrial smog hung over much of the fifty-mile

swath carved for the metropolis from the swamps and jungles of the Ganges delta. the road was bordered by water-filled ditches where women flailed laundry, men bathed, children played.

Sacred Brahmani cows strayed into the way and the Sikh honked furiously. Buzzards and vultures perched atop billboards beckoning travelers to fly BOAC or Pan Am. Durell noticed shanties crowded under the protection of the billboard walkways; further away were thatch dwellings amid palms, then moss-green jungle walls.

The air reeked of heat and humidity, rot and vegetation.

A leopard might still be found in these environs. Jackals roamed the suburbs, killing an occasional indigent at night, and crocodiles sometimes snatched a bather or cow in the Hooghly, an overburdened arm of the divine Ganges River that had nourished Calcutta since its founding by British merchants almost three hundred years ago.

Muncie came back to the topic. "But what if you thought I was on the other side?" she asked.

He regarded her quizzically, wondering if she really wanted to hear the answer. "Let's drop it," he told her.

"You're awfully quiet." She took a compact from her purse.

"I'm saving my breath," he said morosely.

She looked tired, with a hint of circles under her blue eyes, even though she'd napped aboard the plane most of the night. It was about seven in the morning now, and although it was only March, the day would be a scorcher. He held his suit jacket on his knees and loosened his tie and collar. They hadn't even managed a fresh change of clothing before leaving Switzerland—their suitcases had vanished with Nuri. So they were not only hot, but grimy. Their heavy coats lay on the seat between them, as alien to this climate as space suits. The bullet crease in Durell's arm burned.

"Let's go shopping," Muncie said. "If I don't get out of these things, I'll go crazy."

"Maybe later," he said.

"Can't you let up for a moment?"

"I can let up when I've done my job. Do what you like when that's finished."

She looked into the compact mirror, lipstick poised. "Is that your way of telling me you're ditching me when you're finished with me?" With bitter humor, she added, "My mother warned me about guys like you."

"I'm not thinking beyond finding your husband," he said.

The street became increasingly congested. There were battered double-decker buses, people clustered on them like bees on a hive. There were rickshaws with jingling bells, trucks and private cars, trolleys and bullock carts and the ever-present cows, strolling between tram tracks to munch the trash of coconut husks thrown away by drink vendors.

Pedestrians were everywhere, crowding the streets and spilling off the sidewalks. Men and women dressed western style or Indian, in *saris* and *chadars* and *astrakhan* caps and grubby, makeshift turbans.

Shopkeepers squatted cross-legged on the counters of their tiny arcade shops, some with another ragged businessman plying his wares from space rented under their counters. Coolies staggered along carrying enormous bundles. Office workers gripped briefcases.

Here and there Durell discerned the almost skeletal form of someone sick or dying—maybe of starvation—on the sidewalk. Only the closest kin would notice the loss in a city with the world's worst poverty and highest population density. They said it was home to a million beggars.

The beggars shuffled and squirmed everywhere, showing their stumps, their blind eyesockets, whining. . . .

Muncie rolled up her window in spite of the heat.

They threaded through ranges of dingy walkup flats. The hammer and sickle had been painted on a wall. Gradually the featureless blocks gave way to older buildings interspersed with red brick factory walls that might have been hauled intact from Scotland. Durell recognized other legacies of the British Raj in the birthday-cake buildings of quasi-Victorian, bastardized oriental architecture.

And everywhere, squatters had a toehold, camping wherever the flow of people allowed an eddy, their few belongings piled in doorways as they cooked *chapatis* over a fire on the sidewalk.

The taxi came to a halt before a three-story apartment house with paint peeling from its stucco sides. An outdoor staircase was visible through wooden latticework. Down the street was the muddy Hooghly, busy with hay boats and junks, ferries and freighters. There was an odor of cremation in the air, blown from the burning *ghats* above the Howrah Bridge.

Fending off beggars and street urchins, Durell told the driver to wait, and took Muncie into the building with him. He was determined not to let her out of his sight on the street.

He never forgot that the Russians would take her, if they could; that Calcutta, with its swarming poverty, was a communist stronghold.

A slight, dark-skinned man named Ajoy Gupta, a K Section operative, welcomed them into his two-room home on the third floor of the building. "Sri Durrelji! Long time!" He extended a wiry hand. He wore a short-sleeved white shirt and khaki slacks. His face was eager and intelligent.

Durell introduced him to Muncie, then took him onto the roof, leaving her to contemplate the outdated calendars that decorated his walls.

Before leaving Switzerland, Durell had used Nuri's transmitter to brief Washington as to his destination, although not his exact purpose—he didn't even trust code with that information. Codes were broken every day—or bought—or stolen.

So Gupta, through Washington, had known to expect him. Trouble was, merely contacting a man like Gupta exposed one to jeopardy. Foreign nationals tended to be lax and poorly motivated. The security problems were legion. The roof was the only safe place to talk with him.

Durell took a rare cigarette from a week-old pack and lighted it, cupping the match against the breeze. He gave one to Gupta, who accepted it gratefully in lips stained red by betel nut juice. "Ah, American! I am an educated man, as you know, but even I cannot afford them anymore.'' He puffed lightly, making it last. Durell gave him the pack. "*Shukreva.*" Gupta thanked him.

Hungry crows flew overhead. The sun bored into Durell's face. "You had word from Washington?" he asked.

"Yes. Nothing is changed. I'm sorry, no elaborate."

It was all he needed. There was still time, but no one knew how much. "*Atcha.*" Durell drew on his cigarette, thinking. "Do you know the Little Sisters of Mercy?" he asked.

"I'm sorry, no."

"It's a religious group, Christian nuns. They have a shelter for the sick."

Gupta nodded wisely. "There are many charitable organizations in Calcutta, Durellji. They come, they go."

Durell gave him a wad of rupee notes. "This is for expenses," he told him. Gupta began babbling his gratitude, and Durell interrupted him. "Use it to take a taxi and follow me—any extra is yours." There would be lots extra—Durell judged it would keep him interested. "I need a backup. You have a gun? Bring it with you. Mrs. Plettner is taking me to the Little Sisters of Mercy, where I must apprehend a man, her husband. Don't ask questions. He isn't likely to be alone, and it may be difficult. Let me go in first and follow when you can without anyone thinking we're together. Keep in the background unless you're needed."

They got Muncie and went down to the street to find a taxi for the Indian. Then they set off for Mother Mary's shelter, which Muncie remembered vaguely as being off Bellagata Road. It was among the *bustee* slums near Circular Canal.

They were half an hour getting there. Traffic was at a crawl, the pith-helmeted police in the intersections virtually overwhelmed.

Durell remembered that Calcutta was a city of slums. Over a third of its population were slum dwellers, and that didn't include people sleeping on the street or in train terminals.

They passed low brick huts built for factory workers, where a hundred people might share one outdoor hydrant and a couple of outdoor toilets.

Filth overflowed onto the mud, mixing with rainwater and draining into the nearby Hooghly. There the Hindus worshipfully bathed, not only in sewage, but amid the garlands and ashes of their cremated dead.

Durell had lost sight of Gupta's taxi. He swore and ordered his driver to pull over to wait. When several minutes passed and Gupta still hadn't emerged from the jostling throng of animals, people, and vehicles, he told the Sikh cabbie to drive on. He knew he was acting recklessly, but his impatience had become almost impossible to quell.

The loss of Sri Gupta wasn't the only disappointment: Muncie, after some meandering, found the place—but it was vacant.

They stood on the bustling sidewalk in the heat with *kangali* street orphans badgering them. "This is it. How could I forget it?" Muncie said, viewing the turreted, Gothic house.

Durell looked back, hoping to see Gupta. The gutter smelled of feces and was black with flies.

Muncie was defensive. "It was five years ago, for heaven's sake. Anything can happen in five years." Her face was flushed with the heat.

Durell pointed to one of the urchins molesting them for a job. *"Ha-ji, sahib?"* the boy said. He had rogue's eyes, cunning and unafraid.

"Do you know where the nuns went?" Durell showed him five rupees.

"Ha, sahib, I know," the boy said.

"Can you direct me to them?"

The child looked at him blankly.

"Can you show me where they are?" Durell asked.

"Ha, sahib!"

"Then get in the taxi."

They drove until the sun's rays beat down from straight overhead and the cows hid in the shade. By then it was clear that the boy merely *wished* he knew where the nuns were.

With a disgusted sigh, Durell gave him a rupee and put him on the street again, then sought the air-conditioned comfort of a Park Street restaurant. He and Muncie shared cold beer and *bekti*. The perch was the first meal they'd eaten since the previous day.

"What now?" she questioned. "Can I buy some new clothes? There are some beautiful shops on this street."

"Rich man's turf," he told her. "I can't have you out there drawing attention to yourself. The Great Eastern Hotel has a shopping arcade. I'll take you there, and we can get a room as well. Kill two birds."

Her hand came over his, a small, cool touch. "Sam, I'm not sure we should share a room. It isn't that I don't want to. . . ." She dropped her gaze.

"You don't owe me any explanations," he said. "You're entitled to your feelings."

"It's just that . . ."

"You're a married woman?"

"I suppose you're wondering why I should let that bother me now. Are you making fun of me?"

"I wouldn't do that. Some people take a while to know what they want."

"Thank you," she said quietly.

"But we still have to share a room." He paid the waiter. "I'm not going to let you out of my sight any more than I have to," he said.

"Oh, is business all you think about? Don't you ever let up?" She rose angrily.

Outdoors the sunlight was blinding, and it was reflected off cars and windshields. He sensed something wrong, then saw the two white men lounging in front of a newsstand.

They were bull-necked, with meaty shoulders and florid faces, and they wore identical full-cut suits of a dark, tropical-weight material.

Two peas out of the same KGB pod. He could tell a mile away.

When he glanced back, they were following him.

Chapter 19

"What's the rush?" Muncie complained.

"No rush," Durell replied, but he kept his hand against the small of her back, urging her along a little faster.

He pretended to ignore the KGB men following them as they passed the spire of the Ochterlony Monument commemorating the British annexation of Nepal.

He supposed he'd been followed since leaving Gupta's flat. At least there was nothing to fear as long as they kept their distance.

He took Muncie into the Great Eastern, registered as Mr. and Mrs., and they then went shopping. This time the Russians weren't visible, but it made him feel no better. They were somewhere on the fringes, waiting their chance.

Returning to their room, Durell locked the door and barracaded it, propping a chair under the doorknob. When Muncie had showered, it was his turn. He cleaned the bullet wound on his forearm with hydrogen peroxide and applied antibacterial salve and a gauze dressing acquired in the hotel's pharmacy.

Muncie was napping when he came out of the bathroom, but Durell couldn't have slept if he'd showered in chloroform.

He was concerned for Gupta and wondered if the Russians had arranged his disappearance. He tried calling Gupta's apartment, but got no answer. Gupta aside, Dr. Plettner was the real issue. Would the whole "Mother Mary" lead turn out to be a ruse? And would Durell find Plettner in time to stop him from striking again?

His hope was that the Russians didn't know Plettner was in Calcutta, that they still were sidetracked onto Muncie. If the KGB got Plettner behind the Iron Curtain, he'd never be heard from again—but his mind would be enslaved to the purposes of world communism.

He was torn between the urge to hurry and the sensible necessity of giving Muncie time to rest. He eyed her still form impatiently. She lay on her back, hips twisted to the side, legs curled. A little-girlish strand of hair fluttered over her parted lips as she breathed.

He didn't know how long he'd sat there waiting, when he was startled by a knock on the door.

"Who's there?" He heard the bed and looked around as Muncie stirred, pulling her skirt down primly over her knees. Her eyes were drowsy.

"It's me, *sahib,* Gobi of the *kangali.*" The voice was a boy's. The street orphans had been known to do almost anything for pay, and it crossed Durell's mind that this could be a setup.

"What do you want?"

"Let me in." The child lowered his tone. "What I have for you is worth *pahntach* rupees."

"Five rupees?" Durell removed the chair and reached for the latch.

"Every boy in the street knows you will pay five rupees for taking to sisters," Gobi announced. He was a smiling, skinny kid with a street-wise swagger.

Durell told Muncie to get her shoes on.

"Five rupees, please?" The boy held out a grubby hand. He might have been ten, but his eyes said forty.

"Not so fast, Gobi. Take me to the sisters first—then I'll give you the money."

The boy shrugged. "*Atcha*. Come, then."

There was the problem of Russian surveillance to deal with. For that Durell sent Gobi to recruit a gang of his peers to surround and obstruct the KGB spies as he left the building.

It worked, and Gobi met them a block away, laughing at the mischief he'd created. "This way," he said, skipping ahead.

They went past the old East India Company Writers Building to Strand Road and Howrah Bridge. Ungainly and immense, the structure spanned the turbulent Hooghly above masts and funnels from all over the world. Its shadow fell on stone *ghats* where women beat their washing and the faithful drank and bathed. The bridge roadway was jammed with traffic and the walkways were packed with pedestrians.

Across the river, Howrah had roughly a million inhabitants and no public sewers. India's biggest train station was over there, where passengers camped and cooked and the less fortunate scavenged and often died.

It would be a good hunting ground for such as the Little Sisters of Mercy, Durell thought.

His thoughts were yanked back by a shout from Gobi, who'd gone a few feet ahead of him in the throng.

The boy was calling for help. Now Durell saw that he was struggling with a man.

"Do something!" Muncie cried.

Durell was already elbowing his way through the crowd. A thug in a green shirt had gotten hold of the raggedy child and seemed intent on dragging him across the roadway. Gobi's frightened eyes caught sight of Durell. "Help, *sahib!* Help Gobi!" he screamed.

All Durell could think of were the child snatchers for which the city was notorious, men who mutilated children and enslaved them as beggars or sold them into prostitution and the pornography industry.

He reached out and grabbed the assailant by the collar,

jerking him back, and the man bared a knife, snarling. The crowd shrank back with cries of alarm. Gobi darted to Durell's side, dancing with excitement. Durell feinted, lunged for the man, and dodged as the bright blade whirred past him in a backhanded stroke. For the instant that Durell was off balance, the Indian turned and darted like a weasel through the mob of people.

"You okay?" Durell asked Gobi.

"Sure, *sahib*, sir."

"Where's Muncie?" Dread shot through him like electricity: She was nowhere to be seen. Now it struck him that the snatching of Gobi had been a diversion—someone had grabbed her while he was busy saving the boy.

He took off after the man in the green shirt, aware that Gobi was at his heels but caring only for Muncie's safety. The only way to find her was to catch Gobi's assailant and force him to talk.

The crowd was a great current that he had to battle, pushing and battering against them, as sweat ran down his face and his breast burned for breath.

Then he was off the bridge. He got a glimpse of the green shirt crossing traffic and heading upriver along the bank.

Durell dodged trucks and buses with bleating horns, got across, and saw the Indian bound past a billboard for Gold Flake cigarettes and turn into an alley. Following, he found himself in a fetid passageway, feet slapping in black muck. He came out behind Howrah Station, the enormous structures of a major railyard on one side, the river on the other.

He didn't know what had happened to Gobi, but he didn't worry about him for the moment. The danger to him was over, and the boy could seek him out again at his hotel.

But Muncie . . .

He might never see her again.

He was running through a flyblown tent town. Dogs and crows picked at heaps of garbage. Broken pots lay scattered like pieces of skulls among rusting rails. People watched him run past without interest. In the haze beyond stood multi-storied buildings.

He was gaining on the man in the green shirt.

There was another sudden turn and he faced the black shadow of a doorway.

He ran through and was struck by the stench of rancid meat and other hot, foul odors that came from large vats. Grinding machines clattered amid piles of bones that were stacked to the ceiling, and the concrete floor was slippery with grease.

It was fat from stewed bones.

He was in a fertilizer factory, where gaunt workers sweated in incredible heat and filth. Flies swarmed in the steamy light, blotting the windows.

Something hit him as he came out the door. There was a paralyzing blow to the side of his head, and he went down rolling. Nothing stopped him from going over a stone embankment and splashing into the stinking bog of a Hooghly beach.

He reeled onto his feet, wiping mud from his face, and looked up to see the green shirt and half a dozen other thugs jeering him.

Then they started throwing the bricks.

He was too out of it to dodge, even if he could have moved fast enough in the slime. Instinct had him reach inside his jacket for his revolver, but one of the bricks numbed his shoulder before he found the gun.

Another one came at his face like a cannonball.

It silenced everything. . . .

Hammers pounded in his head.

His first emotional response was despair.

Even in the confusion of regaining consciousness, he was aware of failure. He'd lost Muncie . . . he'd lost Gobi . . . Plettner seemed as unattainable as a mirage.

Hands touched his face . . . he didn't want to bother opening his eyes, but they wouldn't leave him alone. As he came more fully awake he smelled the foul river mud, heard boat horns, distant traffic—all the sounds of the vast oriental city.

He remembered the bricks, heard himself groan.

Cobwebs befuddled his vision.

He forced himself to comprehend and saw a twilight sky

where the last instant of day drained into a pool of bloody fire. Fort William was a squat black shape on the enormous park across the river.

It was night. Lights shone on boats and ships; fires winked where people cooked on the *ghats* and in back streets. Reflections rippled on the river.

Someone was bending over him, wiping the mud away.

Her voice was surprised. "You are a white man!"

"Who are you?" he asked.

"Sister Teresa, thank you. Of the Little Sisters of Mercy."

Chapter 20

They went as fast as Durell could get the nun and her Indian helpers to go. He didn't tell her he'd come for Dr. Plettner.

"You are most fortunate I found you when I did," Sister Teresa told him. She had a pretty, ascetic face and spoke with a French accent. "Thieves and brigands of all sorts roam the river at night; they'd as soon slit your throat as pluck a chicken. It's our calling to venture out and find the fallen— and we find so many, every day. But not westerners, not Americans!"

Durell saw no reason to go into detail. "I don't know exactly what happened. Somebody must have hit me over the head."

"We'll have a look at it when we reach the shelter. Better see if you still have your wallet, m'sieur."

"I have it," he said, taking it out and looking inside.

"And your money?"

"Yes. All of it."

"Most strange."

"It's a strange world, sister."

They had arrived at a high wattle fence where an Indian girl opened a gate for them. "Just a minute," Durell told them. Across the street, in the hazy radiance of a street lamp, stood Sri Gupta.

"Durellji. You are late," Gupta said as Durell came to him.

"And you, my friend, are patient. How did you find it?"

"I know many people," Gupta said. "I ask until I find. Your head . . . ?"

"It'll be all right. The opposition got Mrs. Plettner."

"I'm sorry—if I'd been there . . . but my taxi got separated in the traffic. . . ."

Durell sighed. "Not your fault," he said. "Nothing to do but pick up and go on. You know what to do?"

Gupta nodded, and Durell returned to Sister Teresa. They went through the gate and into an old *godown* that probably had served the tea clippers. "We have so much room now," she told him. "Our previous quarters were quite cramped."

Row upon row of emaciated patients—most of them men, because men came from the hinterlands to work in Calcutta— lay on low cots waiting to die. Little could be done for most of them, considering the primitive conditions and scarce supplies. "At least we can give their final hours some dignity," Sister Teresa said.

Nuns in white linen habits moved among the sick, feeding, doctoring, cleaning.

"We find them on the street. No one cares but us," Sister Teresa told him.

Looking back, he saw Gupta slip inside, keeping his distance in the gloom.

He said: "I'd like to see your mother superior."

"Mother Mary? She isn't receiving at this hour, m'sieur."

"Wouldn't she, if it were to accept a contribution? I'm very favorably impressed with your work, sister." Durell looked about and felt a wave of nausea as an attendant picked dead flesh from a gangrenous leg. Around him, collapsed bodies showed the ravages of starvation, dysentery, cholera, tuberculosis. . . .

"M'sieur! A donation?" The pretty little nun clasped her hands, her face glowing. "Come this way."

Crossing the warehouse, Durell had a moment to wonder if Mother Mary would tell him where to go to find her brother. If she wouldn't, how could he force her to? After all, Biner had been a go-between for Plettner and Muncie, because Plettner hoped to avoid being located. Did Mother Mary know that?

He chewed his lip worriedly as they approached an office cubicle. He was consoled by one thought: surely if she knew the truth. . . .

"Here we are, m'sieur." Sister Teresa knocked discreetly.

"Come in." The voice was cool but firm.

He entered and found a frail woman who showed the ravages of poor diet and exhaustion in her sunken cheeks and trembling handshake. She obviously took almost nothing for herself. Great dark eyes that stared at him unblinkingly expressed an implacable will and faith. He saw in them no hint of selfishness or cunning, and he knew suddenly, with intense satisfaction, that she would sacrifice her brother to the greater good as readily as she had sacrificed herself.

On being introduced, he wasted no time. "I didn't come in here to give your order money, Reverend Mother. . . ."

"Then Sister Teresa has made a mistake—"

"I misled her deliberately."

"Oh? Are you playing games with us, after she may have saved your life? Please excuse me; my time is limited." She turned back to a letter she had been writing.

"I came to Calcutta to find your brother," Durell told her. It was just luck that Sister Teresa brought me here; I would have come on my own soon enough."

Mother Mary gave him a scolding glare. "So you found out he's here—"

"Here? In this building?"

"I suppose you're a journalist?"

"No, I'm an agent of the U.S. government." He waited to see her reaction and was surprised by its mildness.

"Then it must be important," she said.

"Please, don't try to keep me from him."

"Why on earth would I do that?" She turned to the other nun. "Sister Teresa, be so kind as to take Mr. Durell to my brother."

He walked out of the office stunned by the ease of it and not quite able to believe it. Thoughts raced through his mind: Was it possible there had been a switch of identities? That the man he was about to meet would be someone other than Muncie's husband? Could Biner have conspired to misdirect him with his last breath?

Sister Teresa led him down the long floor, between aisles of patients and busy nuns, toward the river end of the *godown* that extended out over the water. There she stopped where the building had been partitioned. With a wave of her hand, she invited him to proceed without her.

"I'm sorry, I'm not allowed to enter," she said.

His pulse quickened with anticipation as he advanced toward a door, then the sign leapt out at him. In English and other languages, it read:

WARNING
LEPROSY
DO NOT ENTER!

Chapter 21

Durell stared at the sign, then looked back at Sister Teresa.

"You may go in," she said gently—as if that were the question.

He didn't bother to express his reservations.

Of course, if a man wanted to hide, there couldn't be a better place to do it. It challenged Durell's last reserves of determination to grasp the doorknob and turn it.

Lanterns cast a smoky light over a horrible picture of despair. The loathsome disease flaunted its work in the bloody stumps of fingers, arms, legs, running sores, and disfigured faces. Two nuns worked here, one elderly and wizened, the other young and intense. And there was a man. · . . .

The man stooped over the misshapen form of a child already scarred beyond recognition. He saw Durell's shoes. Not raising his eyes, he said, "They brought this one in this evening. Abandoned some time ago, by the look of him. Another night and the dogs or jackals would have carried him off." The man's voice was tired and woeful.

"Mightn't it have been better if they had?" Durell asked. He found himself holding his breath against the stench.

"It's not for me to decide," the man replied. "It's a life, and I'm here to save lives."

Durell's reply stuck in his throat as the man looked up at him. He'd been about to ask whether that was true, and if so, why he'd conspired to kill so many others. But when Durell saw the face, his combativeness left him. The face crushed his doubts, for it was illuminated by the fires of sacred commitment and the humility to die for it.

In that moment Durell was forced to recognize that he'd found Dr. Peter Plettner . . . and to admit that he *must* have been pursuing the wrong man, after all.

He'd thought he was on the verge of ending the *X. coli* threat, but now, standing in the repugnant miasma of sickness and death, he was overcome by hopelessness.

Surely the madmen who'd eluded him would release their plague before he could find a new trail.

He'd done his best. With that thought, he sought to buy a moment's peace of mind—but it didn't come.

Quitting went against his training and everything he stood for.

Instead of peace, he felt anger and then resentment. *X. coli* had originated in Plettner's lab, and if it hadn't been for Plettner's experiments, over a thousand people would still be alive.

Suddenly furious, he yanked Plettner up and threw him against the wall. The nuns yelled and pulled at Durell's jacket; he brushed them away and pushed his face close to the other man's. Plettner looked astonished, frightened. "Who are you? What are you doing?" he pleaded.

"More important, I know who you are—no saint! And I know what you were up to in your lab." Durell's irises had turned from blue to a terrible, stormy black.

"What do you mean?" Plettner asked.

"I mean the stuff you brewed that was used for mass murder—that someone is using now to extort the government of the United States."

"M-murder?" Plettner's face paled to a sallow yellow. He seemed afraid to struggle against Durell. His eyes lit with comprehension. "You found out about the bacteria! It's why I left—believe me! I don't know what's happened since. . . ."

Durell twisted the man's collar tighter, watching his eyes panic. "Tell me about it," he growled.

Plettner clawed the wall, sucking for breath. Durell loosened up a bit. "Please . . . I didn't want to develop the bacteria. Caske forced me to."

"Caske?" Durell hesitated. "He knew what kind of thing you had?"

Plettner nodded. "He kept after me, pressuring me. It was the only way to save the company—to save my reputation as well as his. . . ."

"What was?"

Plettner's face crumpled in woe. "A biological weapon—for germ warfare. He said nobody need know—as long as we looked prosperous they wouldn't ask. He said he could find buyers. . . ." The scientist read the hatred in Durell's face. "I didn't intend to do it—and the discovery was an accident . . . but once Caske found out about it. . . !"

"Of course, you kept it on hand, had to experiment with it, see what it could do, didn't you? That wasn't Caske's fault, was it!"

Plettner's hand covered his eyes. "No. I could have destroyed it, but I didn't, God help me. Instead, when it seemed that Caske really might find a buyer, I was so appalled by what I'd done, I ran away. Maybe my nerves broke . . . maybe I went crazy. But I had to prove to myself that I couldn't have done what Bernhard Caske—and I—had contemplated—that I wouldn't have had any part in plunging the world into the nightmare of biological warfare." He took a breath, struggling with his emotions. "So I came here, trying to make amends. Doing good. And I brought the key to my work with me—here." He tapped his head. "So that no one could ever reproduce what I'd done."

A familiar voice came from behind Durell. "Yes? Well, that does make it convenient now, doesn't it."

It was Ronald Durso.

He stood in the shadows at the rear of the room. Beside him was the railing of a stairway that led through the warehouse floor to the river. He held a pistol on them.

"You!" Plettner cried. "You must have taken the bacteria. . . ."

Now Durell saw the simplicity of his own error: He'd assumed the culprit would be in hiding, but Durso had flaunted his presence openly. "You weren't working with Plettner at all. And you didn't kill Biner to protect Plettner from me, but because you wanted to get to him first for your own purposes."

"Very good," Durso said, smirking, "but a little late, Mr. Durell." He waved the gun toward the stairs. "Now, if you will both accompany me?"

"Look out, Durellji!"

Durell hurled himself aside, hoping he was faster than Durso's aim. As he hit the floor, he heard Gupta and Durso exchange shots. Rolling, he came up with his .38 and fired from a crouch. Durso staggered, cursed, tried to level the barrel of his revolver on Durell.

Durell's second shot sent a round through the man's heart.

Durell rose from his crouch and holstered his gun with a hand that felt unsteady. His heart still pounded as he frowned down at Durso's crumpled body. Only dimly was he aware that people were screaming and crying. The lepers were fleeing into the main shelter, raising havoc.

He came back as Gupta touched his arm. "Thanks," Durell told him.

"We'd better leave here," Gupta said.

"Yes. Wait." Durell turned to Dr. Plettner. The man stared at him wide-eyed; he didn't seem to have moved. Durell's thoughts went to Muncie: He doubted the U.S. would ever get her back from the Russians. It seemed that the only safe course would be for the U.S. to employ Dr. Plettner to manufacture the germs and their vaccine just in case the Russians proceeded with *X. coli* research on what information they could force from Muncie. She might know more than she thought she did. At least this way, Durell thought, the

U.S. would have the edge of a head start. "I'm sorry," he told Dr. Plettner, "you'll have to return to the United States with me."

"But . . . isn't it over now?" Plettner asked.

Another voice came from the direction of the stairs. "It's hardly over yet," it said.

Again, Durell realized with alarm, it was a voice he recognized. . . .

Chapter 22

Bernhard Caske peered through the stair railings. He was not alone, and one of those with him was Luis Alegra. Alegra carried an Uzi submachine gun and looked eager to use it.

"My men will relieve you of your weapons," Caske announced. "Quickly, please."

Durell and Gupta had no choice. They surrendered their weapons and were ordered down the stairs, along with Dr. Plettner.

"You were behind everything," Durell said.

"Too bad for you," Caske said, smiling through his beard with a sinister leer. "I thought you had me when you came to me in Geneva. You can imagine my relief when you only wanted my help." He chuckled and added smugly, "You should have struck a bargain with me then, as I suggested. It would have saved you lots of trouble. Into the boat, please "

A power launch was moored at the bottom of the stairs.

Water lapped and flashed among pilings. The sounds of bedlam still came from the confusion above.

"Where are you taking us?" Plettner demanded.

"To a nice, quiet place I've prepared for you downriver, Herr Doctor. We've had you under surveillance until it was ready. When Mr. Durell arrived, we, of course, had no alternative but to act immediately, so you may find a few things not yet in place. The setting is sure to be conducive to your work—I do hope we can be friends again." The boat had started down the river.

"I'll never work for you," Plettner replied.

Caske's laugh said everything about him. It was condescending . . . evil . . . insane. "We shall see about that," he told Plettner. "After all, you owe me for ruining my company and making a fool of me."

"You made a fool of yourself, with your overstated claims. If you'd just given me some breathing space . . ." Plettner said remorsefully.

"Shut up your driveling!" Caske barked. "You had a chance to do things your way. Now you will do them mine."

Durell broke in. "Which means that he's to supply you with the means to do whatever you please with the rest of the world."

"Exactly, my friend." Caske raised his cunning eyes to the night sky. "It could all have been accomplished by now without this bother, if only Dr. Plettner had left a more substantial amount of the culture behind. Unfortunately, we used nearly all of it on that cruise ship demonstration—your government really should have come across on the strength of that, you know. What was left in the laboratory wasn't enough for our aims, even if it hadn't been destroyed by your meddling." He rubbed his hands and smiled wickedly. "Oh, well, it all will be set right very soon. Am I correct?"

Plettner made no reply.

"You're sicker than those wretches we left in the nuns' shelter," Durell said.

"I get what I want!" Caske shouted. "Tie them up!"

Leaving Calcutta behind, they followed the winding Hooghly south through the immense swamp and jungle that formed the

Ganges delta. Night cloaked the countryside. The river buoys and ocean-going vessels were the only signs of civilization.

Durell couldn't guess how far they had gone when the boat abruptly slowed and angled for shore. They tied up at stone stairs that rose out of the river. With the boat's motor dead, the air was alive with the racket of insects and frogs.

The prisoners were led ashore and into the compound of an abandoned river palace. Its crumbling, vine-entwined stone buildings sported the tiered domes and pierced crenelations of classical Indian architecture.

The odors of the river mixed with the ripe fragrance of wild fruits and freshly cut grass.

Bare lightbulbs powered by a generator Durell heard chuffing beyond the walls illuminated the interior, where a sizable number of Indian hirelings camped. Lianas thick as Durell's arm probed among the lotus-bundle columns and Moghul windows.

In a larger room that might have served as a reception chamber were more men, clearly Indian laborers involved in restoring the place. Here technicians also were putting the final implements of a modern laboratory in place. Tina was there.

"I believe you know each other?" Caske intoned.

Durell saw what might have been love light up Plettner's sad eyes. "Tina. . .?"

She turned away from him without showing the least interest and took Caske's arm. "I see everything went as planned," she said.

Durell felt sure she'd been dragged here against her will by Ron Durso. He wasn't sure what she had up her sleeve, but he didn't buy the act. Caske seemed to. Plettner certainly did: He looked crushed.

"We had a misfortune," Caske told her. "I'm afraid your dear husband made the highest sacrifice. You will never see him again." He patted her hand.

She gasped and turned away, burying her face in her hands.

Plettner spoke to her from a distance. "Tina, dear . . . he wasn't worth your grief . . . believe me. . . ."

She faced him with angry, dry eyes. "I won't miss him," she said firmly. "And I don't need you, buster. Mr. Caske will take care of me just fine, right, honey?" She took the bald man's arm.

"You may rely on me," he said smoothly. "Go now and rest for dinner."

When she was gone, he turned to Plettner. "Such a charming child, don't you think?"

"Send her away, you swine," Plettner groaned. "She doesn't know what she's doing, and you are incapable of feeling. You'll only use her."

Caske looked amused. "I'm afraid I must admit that you're right, Herr Doctor. I believe you refused to do my bidding; perhaps I can use Mrs. Durso to change your mind."

Plettner looked apprehensive. "W-what do you mean?"

"Perhaps, if I . . . hurt her." Caske gave him a crooked smile.

Plettner drew a short breath. "No . . ."

"I can see the bruises on that beautiful white skin, can't you? Perhaps if she were injured . . . sexually? You see, I know of your liaison with the child . . . your fondness—which she, unfortunately, seems not to reciprocate."

"Please let her go." Plettner sounded deeply shaken and his voice trembled with pleading.

But Caske kept talking. "Yes, something sexual should bring you around, something especially painful and humiliating."

"You inhuman beast!" Plettner screamed. "You wouldn't! Oh, God!" He fell on his knees. "Don't!"

Caske studied the man before him as he would an object that vaguely interested him.

Whatever spirit Plettner had summoned to stand against Caske now all seemed to evaporate. It almost was as if Durell could see the man crumple, like a piece of burning paper.

"You will cooperate?"

"Yes," Plettner replied. "Whatever you say."

Durell had foreseen the end, but had known he was power-less to change it. It had been like watching a dream.

But the bad dream wasn't over. Caske signaled his guards, indicating Durell, and said, "Below with him and his Indian stooge!"

Chapter 23

They kicked Durell and Gupta, their hands still tied behind them, down the stone stairs. When Gupta couldn't get to his feet, Alegra kicked him unconscious, laughing and sweating.

"Leave him be," Durell demanded.

For his effort, he got a knee in the groin. As he doubled over, the pain reaching with dull force through his abdomen and hips, the Puerto Rican caught him by the hair and threw him back against the rusty iron door of a cell.

Durell leaned there, catching his breath and hurting.

Alegra said, "I'm going to have you for lunch, pal. Now get inside!" He opened the cell door, a solid sheet of metal with a six-by-six-inch window punched in it. Durell staggered in. They dragged Gupta in and clanged the door shut.

"You're lucky, Durell," Alegra taunted. "Mr. Caske says you're worth more alive than dead—for now."

Cramps spread in rigid waves through his gut. He caught a movement out of the corner of his eye. Someone was reaching out of the shadows for him.

It was Muncie.

She fell against him, sobbing.

"So it wasn't the Russians after all," he said as she untied him. When his hands were free, he held her tightly.

She had a nasty bruise on her cheek. "Are you all right?" he asked.

She nodded, trying to smile. "Mr. Caske tried to persuade me to assist Peter in the lab, but I wouldn't do it."

Durell slid down the wall and sat in the dust. "I suppose he threatened worse, if you don't?" He heard the sounds of the jungle and the faraway hoot of a ship's horn.

"I can't imagine being tortured," she said. "It seems so medieval."

Durell rubbed his wrists. "Hold out as long as you can," he said.

"Easy for you to say." She sat down beside him and rested her cheek on his shoulder.

He felt the life trembling in her and thought how fragile she seemed.

She gave a bitter laugh. "Are we really talking like this? Sam, I'm scared." She snuggled closer. "Tell me everything will be okay."

"I won't lie to you," he told her. "Whatever happens, your part will be to hold out as long as you can. Any assistance you give might make a difference; every hour of delay may mean an hour of life for others."

"What difference does it make, if the end is the same?" she said resentfully.

"Maybe it'll make a difference in the end," he said.

"If you believe in miracles!" She sighed, pulling herself together. "I'll try, Sam . . . but I'm not counting on the cavalry arriving in the nick of time."

The cell was hot and musty even before the sun had passed above the treetops the next morning. Durell awoke thirsty, and realized he hadn't had anything to drink since the previous afternoon. His mouth tasted as if it had been stuffed with dirty cotton.

They came and took Muncie a few minutes later. She looked very frightened, all the numbing terror of the unknown visible on her face. He could only watch helplessly.

When they were gone, he turned to Gupta. "Let's check the bars on the window," he suggested.

But the Indian couldn't get up. "My back, Durellji; it pains me."

"Ribs?"

"Not ribs—something inside, I think." He raised himself onto his elbows with a groan.

Durell pulled up Gupta's shirt and found massive bruises all over the man's torso, souvenirs of the beating Alegra had given him. "Have we any water?" Gupta asked.

Durell strode to the door. "We need water down here!" he yelled. He thought he may have heard a distant laugh. Then silence. A sickening rage squeezed his stomach like a fist. Crossing back to Gupta, he felt the man's forehead and found it burning with fever. He was probably bleeding internally, with the injuries already infected. "Try to rest," he told him. Gupta winced as he lay back on the floor.

Durell went to the window and pulled himself up by grasping the bars. Outside was a courtyard paved with pitted limestone, surrounded by a wall. The wall was not so high that he couldn't scale it—if he could get to it.

Sweating in the muggy heat, he began to work on one bar, twisting back and forth to loosen it in the plaster. He felt rewarded within a few minutes, when he could turn the bar an eighth of an inch. Bits of rotten plaster began breaking loose, and he brushed them away with growing excitement.

He heard the chattering of a troop of jungle monkeys, the crowing of birds.

In a quarter of an hour, he had loosened the bar so that he could turn it a half-inch and jiggle it up and down. He worked faster, certain that a little more time was all he needed to work the bar completely loose.

Footsteps sounded on the stairs.

Quickly, he packed clods of plaster back around the bar and got away from the window.

It was Caske, with Alegra. The latter carried his slung Uzi and a water pitcher.

"Gupta, they've brought something to drink," he said.

The door opened, and Caske stood before him, smiling. "We heard your call for water. Forgive the delay."

Durell indicated Gupta. "He may have internal bleeding, thanks to your Nazi friend."

"Then he must be very thirsty. Luis?"

Alegra grinned evilly and tilted the pitcher, pouring its contents onto the floor. His eyes were like needles in Durell.

The smell of the fresh water raised a frantic thirst in Durell, but he didn't give Alegra the satisfaction of showing any emotion. Turning to Caske, he said, "What do you want of me?"

Caske replied in a matter-of-fact voice. "People are leverage against other people, Mr. Durell, and leverage means success. In the present case, you'll give me leverage by your suffering." He paused, studying Durell. "Yes, that's all I want of you—your suffering." Caske's eyes turned sinister. "Be so kind as to come with us," he said, stepping aside.

A cold feeling crawled down Durell's spine, but staring at Alegra's Uzi, he knew he had no choice.

They took him outside, to the courtyard he'd seen from his cell. The unaccustomed tropical sun flashed against his eyes with brutal force as he was led across paving stones that were already hot. The destination was a small, sentry-box-style structure made of corrugated metal, freshly painted black. There was no shade anywhere near it.

As they locked him inside, Caske said: "Have a nice day, Durell. Think water."

Pacing the tiny cubicle was a matter of two steps one way, two another; there was barely enough room to sit on the floor. And when he stood up, the hot roof was within an inch of his head. In a little while he'd shrunk down to the center of the chamber, as far from the metal walls as he could get. The sun turned it into an oven.

Hours passed. The air became so suffocatingly hot he felt he dared not breathe it.

Sweat soaked his clothing, lying against his clammy skin without evaporating.

From time to time he heard passing voices, the sawing of wood and hammering of nails.

He tried not to move at all in order to conserve his vitality. Besides, there was no place to hide from the hot metal encasing him.

By noon he was gasping for breath, and by midafternoon, when even the insects hid and the birds no longer sang—when the corrugated tin was too hot to touch and the mere thought of cool water on the tongue was enough to drive Durell crazy—he began hallucinating.

In horrible visions he saw Muncie and Maj. Miller, and his old Grandpa Jonathan and Gen. McFee, the living mixed with the dead, calling from a cool shade beyond a river of flame.

He wanted to go to them, but he couldn't face any more fire.

He was being consumed by fire.

He heard screams that he later realized came from his own mouth.

Then a hornet's buzzing filled his ears, bringing the fire with it, right inside his skull, growing louder and hotter. . . .

A sweet coolness bathed Durell, and he blinked eyelids that were sticky with tears. Hands held him under the legs and arms, carrying him across the flagstones of the courtyard.

Twilight had come.

He tried to speak. His throat was dry, his lips puffed and cracked.

As his senses returned, he was grateful that he'd survived the day.

He didn't see how he could live through another like it.

Even in his condition he could take cunning pleasure in one thought: the memory of the bar he'd loosened that morning. Tonight he'd be free.

They dragged him down the stone stairs and threw him into the cell, leaving without having spoken.

Durell just lay on the floor without moving, relishing the

cool air he breathed. He ran his tongue around his lips. They felt like wads of tissue paper. He couldn't summon enough saliva to swallow—the oven where he'd spent the day had baked him dry.

"Durellji?"

Durell turned his head without lifting it from the floor. "I'm back, Gupta," he croaked.

"It is the end for me, Durellji. I can't move."

"I'm sorry . . ."

"Don't be sad for me. Death is peace. But if I could have a taste of water . . .? The pain is in my kidneys."

The sun had vanished and the only light was indirect, from illumination beyond the door and window. Durell sensed that his strength was slowly reviving. He knew Caske wouldn't supply them with water, but he still had a chance to save Gupta as well as himself. He pulled himself up the wall and made his way to the barred window of the cell. The night was a star-filled purple hanging over the black shapes of wall and jungle.

He gripped the bar he'd worked loose that morning and got a bitter surprise. A half-inch-wide strip of steel had been welded across the bars so that they had to be removed all at once or not at all—an impossible task.

He slumped down, wondering what he would say to Gupta. "Just keep hoping, Gupta," he said. "Gupta?"

There was no reply.

Durell found him in the dark. He was unconscious, his pulse weak.

Durell threw himself at the door. "Water!" he shouted through the peephole. "A man's dying down here. Water, damn you!"

No one responded.

Some time later he heard footsteps coming down the stairs and saw the cell door swing open. Caske was speaking to Muncie in a most courteous way. "I hope you had a pleasant day. I regret that you must return here, but perhaps that won't be for long. When you see the error of your ways, my dear, ask anything, and it shall be yours."

Light from the opening fell across Durell. "You're looking the worse for wear—you must be dreading tomorrow. After all, how many times can one cook the same goose?" Caske said with a malicious laugh. He added soberly, "Mrs. Plettner can spare you that. Why don't you speak with her about it?"

The door clanged shut. "Until tomorrow," Caske called.

Durell spoke through the gloom. "You okay?"

"They didn't touch me. You sound awful."

"Dehydrated. I cooked in a metal box all day."

"Sam, it's my fault!" She sat beside him.

"Why?"

"If I give in and assist Peter in the lab, he'll let up on you."

"Don't do it," he said, his jaw set stubbornly.

"You don't understand. He's working on my—"

"What?"

"He must know . . . I care for you."

Durell said nothing.

"Know what I did today? I swam in the lily pond, while you were being cooked to death!"

"You didn't know. Besides, enjoy whatever you get. Just don't give in," Durell growled.

"I saw Tina. We got to talk a little. I feel sorry for her now," Muncie said. "I guess I never realized how much she loved him."

"Did she tell you that?" he asked in surprise. "When she saw him last night, she acted as if she couldn't have cared less."

"She's just keeping her distance so Caske will trust her with him—it's the only way she could have gotten to see him at all," Muncie said. "She says Peter's deeply depressed, and she doesn't think he'll go through with helping Caske manufacture the bacteria."

Durell's throat ached dryly. "Maybe she doesn't know she's the reason he *will* do it. Caske's told him she'll be the one to pay if he doesn't cooperate."

"Oh, no!" Muncie gasped.

"Plettner's in a no-win situation as a man in love, and he's in a no-win situation as a scientist of conscience," Durell said.

"Then he really loves her. I'm glad. I'm finally free." She almost seemed to be speaking to herself.

Durell said, "If you see her tomorrow, tell her where they're keeping me. It's right out in the open—maybe . . ." He shook his head. "There isn't much hope. I'm only there during daylight, and people are sure to be nearby. But tell her the door's held shut by a hasp; just has a spike through it, no lock."

"I'll tell her, Sam." Muncie was solemn. "Is there no other hope?"

Durell gave an unhappy sigh. "There's always hope—the Russians, for one."

"My God, I'd forgotten about them! Do you think they still—"

"More than ever," he said. "They'll be frantic, and they won't spare any effort to find our trail. The way they see it, we may get a flying head start on a whole new generation of biological weapons. If we have it, they've got to. That's their philosophy in a nutshell."

"Not so different from ours, when you think about it, is it?" she said. He felt her hand on his cheek. "I didn't mean to be glib. . . ." She looked up at him, her face a faint glow in the dark. "Please tell me when you can't take the punishment anymore, Sam."

He took her hand in his. "Fair enough—but if you don't hear from me, you're to stick by your refusal to help them. Clear?"

"Even if it means—the worst?"

"The worst would be for Caske to get what he's after," he replied.

They sat close to each other for a long while.

Frogs chirped in the trees and bellowed down by the river. Ships' horns called across the waters of the Hooghly.

Slowly, through the pain and darkness, Durell became aware of the magnetism of Muncie's body beneath the flimsy fabric of her clothing. The scent of her clean hair and skin was tantalizing, and he sensed the aura of her desire as surely as if it flickered in a fire visible to the eye. Then, out of the darkness, her mouth touched his, and they kissed. Her mouth was wet and sweet as an orange.

Wordlessly, he crushed her against the floor. . . .

Chapter 24

The next morning Gupta was dead, the final result of Luis Alegra's savage beating.

No one troubled to remove the body when they came for Muncie.

Her bitter, dusky eyes didn't part with Durell's until they slammed the door behind her.

Still no water or food for him, though he didn't notice the hunger, only the raging thirst.

He sat against the rough stone wall and stared dumbly at Gupta's body as dizziness played across his mind. His task, he told himself, was to outlive the day. One more day. . . .

He saw his hands where they hung limply between his knees. They didn't feel like his hands—not that they were numb, because they did have feeling. But his senses were becoming disjointed, and what he felt was not necessarily what he saw.

He worked this over in his mind, slowly.

He tried to forget thirst.

"Durell! On your feet!"

Dimly, he regarded the three men filling the open doorway, confused that they had managed to open the door without his being aware of it. Caske was there, as usual, with Alegra and one other, an Indian henchman.

Without hinting at the resolve that at that moment crystallized in his mind, he steeled himself. It wasn't much of a chance, he thought, but it might be the only one he'd get. . . .

He hurled himself from the floor and lurched across the room, arms outstretched for Alegra and the black Uzi he carried, a snarl on the bursting skin of his bleeding lips.

He caught them by surprise.

There was a tangle of arms, knees, and flailing fists as he groped for Alegra's throat amid cries and curses. Then the Indian was swinging on one of his arms, and he saw the barrel of the Uzi coming down on him. He dodged and it missed his head, cracking into his shoulder and numbing it. He reeled back as another blow caught him in the ribs, and then they were all over him as he sank to his knees.

"Enough!" Caske roared. "I don't want to lose him yet. Bring him out."

They put him in the box.

For hours the heat consumed him, but the light coming beneath the door told him it still was only midday. The worst hours lay ahead—one o'clock, two o'clock, three o'clock. It would be five before the torment lessened appreciably. He clenched his teeth and his head drooped down from hunched shoulders. There was nowhere to lean without getting burned by the metal walls. He forced each thick, steaming breath of scalding air down his throat and into his parched lungs. Sweat oozed, sucking his body dry. . . .

He thought he'd gag on his swollen tongue.

He'd never feared death, but he hadn't spent much time thinking about it either. For the first time since arriving here, the black reality of his death leered at him. . . .

His only defense seemed to be to stay alert, but he had to fight to keep from blacking out.

He yanked himself awake.

Like a drowning man, he struggled up again.

When he started going under once more, he thought that he may have been weakened too much to fight off the end for a third time. . . .

A tremendous explosion rocked the earth, jolting him wide-eyed. He heard the rattle of debris falling onto the tin roof over him.

There were screams, shouts, the confused sound of people running.

Someone was removing the spike that held the door closed, and he scrambled out, strengthened by new hope.

"Mr. Durell?"

The door opened, and Durell blinked unbelievingly. "Tina!"

In the background he saw Caske's men milling in confusion. Many were injured; others were trying to organize a fire brigade. Dense smoke laden with the searing fumes of burning chemicals swirled through the courtyard. Fire was spreading through the wing of the palace that Durell remembered was over the cell where he'd been held prisoner. He took it all in instantly. Then Tina. Her pretty face was a white mask, her eyes rimmed with red. There was a burn slash on her left arm and a rose of dark blood matted in her copper hair.

She thrust a quart bottle into his hands. "It's a bomb, Mr. Durell. Peter said to give it to you—you'd know what to do." Her voice caught with a sob, but she controlled it. "Peter blew himself up!" she added.

So Dr. Peter Plettner had found a solution after all, Durell thought. By killing himself, he'd killed the secret of *X. coli*.

There came another explosion and more screams. Chunks of stone and plaster smashed into the courtyard as shrieking birds fluttered away in the jungle.

"Where's Caske?" Durell asked.

"I saw him take Muncie into the basement. He's probably scared she'll get loose in the confusion. Don't let him get away, Mr. Durell!"

He was moving before she'd finished talking, his eyes fixed on the door. His legs moved sluggishly, and he had the hellish feeling of being mired in a dream, but he wouldn't be denied. At least no one paid him any heed in the flaming bedlam.

Only the bomb in his hand gave him any hope of an advantage—he knew he wouldn't survive a hand-to-hand struggle, and he had no other weapon. His coordination was gone for the time being.

He came to the doorway and rested a second against the frame. The flames in the palace made a windy roar. Tine waited behind him. He took a breath and went in, stumbling on the stairs but catching himself. Cautiously he descended, recognizing with distaste the odors of the dungeon.

Then he saw Caske, and Caske saw him. Alegra was there, too, and both were armed.

As in Geneva, Caske had the dangerous look of a wounded beast. Durell took in the gun and the ugly snarl and knew the next thing would be a shot. . . .

Without thinking he threw the bottle and flattened himself back inside the stairwell. Nearly simultaneously he heard Caske fire once.

There was a blinding flash that sucked the air from his lungs, and he felt a crushing force that was beyond sound, beyond comprehending.

His ears rang, and dust filled his nose. He couldn't see.

He coughed as fumes stung his nose and throat, burning his eyes. He called Tina, barely able to hear himself, then saw her legs through the smoke. She lay on the stairs, unmoving.

"Sam?" The voice came muffled by the cell door. "Is that you?"

It was Muncie. "I'll get you out," he yelled. The ancient palm-trunk roof beams were afire. He went down and found what was left of Bernhard Caske and Luis Alegra. There was nothing recognizable, only a mass of shredded meat and guts with the clothing burned off and the heads and extremities blasted away. An iron ring with the cell key hung from a nail in the wall. He grabbed it and let Muncie out. Gupta's body still lay on the floor in there. He'd just have to leave it.

Muncie rushed into his arms, coughs racking her body.

"Help me with Tina," he said. "This place is going."

"Oh, my God!" She covered her mouth in horror.

"Just step over it and don't look," he said, hustling her past the mutilated remains.

With Muncie's help, he got Tina up the stairs and safely out of the building. His head swam, but he didn't pass out.

Caske's launch was still tied up on mossy pilings beside the *ghat* stairs leading down the riverbank. On the bottom step Durell knelt, shaking, smelling the filth of Calcutta in a river that was also a burying ground, then he gleefully dunked his face and drank.

Life revived in him like an unfolding flower.

"Who's that?" Muncie asked, pointing.

He raised his eyes and saw a freighter, anchored hundreds of yards away, launch a whaleboat loaded with men. Flying from the stern of the ship was the red merchant ensign of the USSR. He rose unsteadily to his feet. "Help me get Tina into the boat. It's the Russians." He cursed under his breath.

Tina was limp, an awkward burden.

He could hear the puttering sound of the whaleboat's engine from far across the water.

The fire still raged.

Tina slid woozily over the gunwale and dropped inside Caske's launch.

"Stay where you are, *pashalta*!" a Russian shouted through a bullhorn. By then Durell had Muncie over the side. Throwing loose the mooring lines, he started the engine.

"Halt, or you will be shot!"

A submachine gun stuttered, and half a dozen rounds sang overhead, clipping leaves from branches.

Durell gave it the gas, spinning the wheel. The fast launch reared like a horse and bolted from the shallows into the broad expanse of midriver. He saw guns sighted on him, but the noise of their firing was drowned out in the roar of his engine.

A picket of white spouts crossed his wake, then he was safely out of range.

A final glimpse over his shoulder showed smoke rising above the tropical riverbank, the anchored freighter, and other ships plodding along in the wilting heat. The whaleboat's bow was in his wake, but was falling further and further behind.

Muncie sat close, her hair trailing in windblown ribbons, and they raced toward freedom. . . .

Durell spent the afternoon submitting a preliminary report through the communications center in the U.S. Consulate on Harrington Street. He learned from Washington that Caske had been on the verge of losing his company to creditors when Plettner vanished. Without the star scientist, Caske's back had been forced to the wall.

Finished with business, a good meal buoying them, Durell and Muncie visited Tina, who'd been hospitalized for observation and rest. Her injuries weren't serious.

"The real hurt was to something they can't bandage," Tina told them. "I . . . I'm sorry for the pain I caused you, but I couldn't help myself . . . and I guess Peter couldn't either." She touched Muncie's hand.

Muncie's smile was bitter. "I'm sorry, too." That was all she said about it.

"I had no idea he'd take his own life." Tina sobbed. She turned to Durell. "Muncie told me where you were, that you'd said you'd help us get loose if there was a way. Peter brought out the bomb; like he'd just been waiting for a chance. He told me to take it to you, and you'd know what to do. After I left, there was this explosion, and I looked back . . . and it was the lab." With pleading eyes, she said, "I feel it made him a hero, don't you?"

"He sacrificed himself," Durell said.

"I never even knew what it was all about," Tina said.

"People get caught in the middle," he told her, remembering another young woman under hospital sheets. Tina was more fortunate than Nydia Duka, whose mind had crumbled under the weight of self-imposed guilt and the horrible memories she'd brought from the *Sun Rover*. Word today had been that she'd gone hopelessly insane.

He drew a long sigh. "It's all over now. It's hard, but you've got to believe you can go on."

"Yes," she said. She turned to Muncie. "Do you think we could help each other?"

Muncie considered it. "Check with me in San Juan in about a week, and I'll let you know." She wrote an address on a slip of paper and handed it to her. Her expression said she might take Tina up on the suggestion.

Then she and Durell left the hospital and were chauffeured away in a consulate limousine.

"So you'll return to San Juan?" Durell said.

"And hopefully my island, when it's safe."

He said nothing for a long moment as they wove through teeming streets headed for Dum Dum airport. Then, "The days's still young. We could catch a Fokker and be in Darjeeling in a few hours. I know a lodge with a view of the sunrise against Kanchenjunga—Everest is only eight hundred feet higher. Let's save our goodbyes for the sunrise. Will you?"

She regarded him warmly. "Of course, dear Sam—" she gave him a peck on the nose, her sultry eyes close to his— "but don't think you're getting away when the sun comes up. Why do you suppose I told Tina not to look me up for a week?"

They kissed, causing the chauffeur to cut his eyes from the road to the rearview mirror . . . again . . . and again . . . and again. . . .